# RECIPE FOR REVENGE

## Hurt People, Hurt People

# TY HENNINGS

# Table of Contents

# Prologue

**May 29, 2024 Salmon Creek, WA**

"One, two, three, GO!" Joey slammed down all of his chocolate milk with one swallow, a technique he and his buddies had perfected over the course of the school year. Victoriously, he was the first to speak. "Done!" he said to Michael, his best friend forever—they'd known each other two whole years.

After losing the daily chug-a-lug, Michael frowned and shrugged with a helping of feigned ambivalence. "Big deal! That was the first time this week. I'll get you tomorrow."

The cafeteria was lined with the obligatory drab yellow bricks from the floor to chest level. There was about as much emotion in the faces of the lunch ladies as nutrients in the tater tots they dutifully handed out, eight per tray, three thousand times. Half the students left three-quarters of their forever-served-and-seldom-enjoyed pepperoni pizza on the tray when they returned it. Thankfully for their physical development and for the school's funding, their servings of "vegetables" had been mostly eaten, attested by the smears of ketchup that were left behind. All in all, lunchtime had been pretty boring, but Joey and Michael were excited. Thursday was gym day, and, even better, today was the moment they had waited for all year: parachute day.

It was all Mr. Wes could do to keep the class single file as he took them to the gymnasium. In jubilant chaos, half of them were whispering or mouthing words to the one in front or behind—partly due to their excitement and partly to see what they could get away with. Michael, in his devilry, turned around and started to make funny faces at Joey to instigate a laugh. Joey, wise to his buddy's old tricks, covered his mouth so his prankster friend wouldn't get him in trouble... again. As he mustered all his strength to hold back a laugh, he felt a strange discomfort in his stomach, a surprisingly strong echo of a stomach flu he thought he'd gotten over a month ago. *Mom said I'm fine*, he thought as he got ready for the major romp.

They entered the gym like a swarm of bees. Mr. Wes almost too willingly relieved himself of the duty of watching the hoodlums and passed them off to Mrs. Branigan, who, as always, was standing straight as a pole wearing a white polo shirt and camouflage shorts. She had a Fox 40 whistle around her neck and a clipboard in her hand. Indeed, she was quite imposing, especially to a second grader, but all the kids knew she was soft at heart... so long as they obeyed the rules.

As they stood in line for roll, everyone's excitement was skyrocketing. This was the most anxious Joey had felt since the Smash Bros. tournament at his birthday party a week ago. *Hurry up!* he thought as Mrs. Branigan got through the letters R and S. Joey's insides were so twisted with excitement, he thought he would hurl, and he could feel his fingers getting tingly with the buzz in the room.

Once the roll was taken, the kids instinctively gathered (some faster than others) around the mystical, circular, rainbow-colored bull's-eye cloth. It was never actually intended for saving someone's life, but it was called a parachute nonetheless, and the name alone made it all the more exciting as the kids imagined gliding through the air being held up by the massive fabric.

Joey took a firm grip on the parachute and looked askance at Mrs. Branigan, waiting for the instructions to make magic with the parachute.

The teacher barked out an order, and the kids all raised their arms and stepped forward in perfect synchrony. As they ducked underneath the fabric they were holding, the parachute formed an amazing mushroom of enormous size, large enough to conceal all thirty-one children and all their laughter. It was awesome, like being inside a tie-dyed balloon.

Underneath the psychedelic canopy, Joey caught a glimpse of Tristan on the other side. She and her friends were beaming with laughter, and she was as beautiful as always. Her face lit up the otherwise darkened pseudo-shelter the class had created. For a moment, they locked eyes, and she smiled at Joey and blushed. His heart was pounding. That simple act that a little girl does with its magical power over little boys was too much for Joey, and her smile blurred along with everything else. *I love her*, he thought—and he loved her so much that the pounding of his heart was now further aggravating his rapidly worsening stomach pain. He had to get his mind off of her so he could settle down, a tall order for a seven-year-old boy so very in love.

The parachute was lifted back up, and the kids came out from under its canopy. Now it was time for the highlight of the event: popcorn. Mrs. Branigan got a huge bag of foam balls from the closet. Joey's excitement mounted and continued to take its toll on his small frame—and coupled with the pounding of his heart for his beloved Tristan, he now had a throbbing headache as well.

After lowering the parachute to the ground, the balls were thrown onto it, and the children raised the sides so as to corral the balls into the center. Mrs. Branigan held up her hand, then dropped it quickly and blew the whistle. The balls went hurtling into the air, rivaling Vesuvius in his rage. Immediately, the convex parachute was distorted into a torrent of undulating waves caused by the children throwing their sections high and low, each at their own amplitude and frequency, like the cacophony of their voices. Some of the spunkier kids were shaking the parachute like crazy. Surprisingly, a few of the kids were hardly moving it at all.

Whenever a ball flew off, Mrs. Branigan yelled out to the child closest to it to run after it, throw it back, then rejoin the circle.

"Sally!" she yelled and blew her whistle. Sally James made a pretty slow advance toward the wayward ball. She looked pale with fear, the way less athletic kids usually do when called upon to catch, kick, or throw. Nonetheless, she picked it up slowly and ventured a throw, but the ball made it only about two feet.

"Girls can't throw!" yelled two boys—and instantly, as if directed by an unforeseen maestro, half the class burst into laughter. Mrs. Branigan did not laugh and started making her way towards the little girl. Turning paler, presumably from embarrassment, Sally began stepping back. Seemingly disoriented, she tottered and stopped. Blinking, she looked at Mrs. Branigan, who was now running towards her. Then Sally fell flat on her face.

Joey couldn't laugh. As he saw her face hit the ground and blood ooze out of her nose and mouth, fear crept into his mind. He felt more lightheaded. He closed his eyes and shook his head in an attempt to get control of his thoughts. He opened them again. *Why did the kids opposite me drop the parachute?* he wondered. His eyes still blurry, he tried to focus and looked harder. *Is that Chris and Tina? Why are they lying face down on the parachute?*

Joey reeled back and forth. The pain in his head and stomach surged as vomit erupted out of his mouth and nostrils, covering his trembling little hands. He closed his eyes and stumbled. The last thing he ever heard was Michael screaming, "Joey!"

# PART I

# CHAPTER 1

# CHANDRA SANDEEP

---

**2006–2007 India**

Inside the bedroom of a meek shanty in rural Tamil Nadu, India, hung a drawing. In its background, a sea-broad crimson sky dotted with grey clouds blanketed a distant orchard. The short-trunked, almost bush-like trees were freckled with people scaling ladders, ostensibly in search of bright yellow and deep red pears, but the secret decoder of a magnifying glass revealed that they were indeed leaving the pears in favor of the much more prized bluish-green knob at its heel. Along the tree line, others hefted satchels and baskets towards a large mound where they dumped out the mysterious small green pods into a pile that rivaled the more distant trees in height. A swarm of people attended this pile, picking at its feet. With a few others to the left, they magically turned the heap into two smaller lumps, one of the same green color and another light khaki.

Though mysterious to those unfamiliar with the agriculture of southern India, nothing was terribly gloomy about this piece. Nonetheless, there was an aura of melancholy about it. Situated directly in the center, zoomed in as it were, the focal point of the drawing was a man's hands with a landscape quite their own. The dark-skinned hands were slightly curled so that both the palms and the backsides of the hands could be seen by the viewer. On the dorsal side, bulging veins streamed down the sinewy hands showing the malnourished strength that came from years of climbing ladders, picking fruit, and carrying countless bushels of the cherished crops harvested on an Indian cashew plantation. Following the contour of the hand to the palm side, one could see the blisters, lesions, calluses, and scars on the fingers that told the beginning of the tale of the difficult and dangerous work of removing the delicious nut from its acidic shell so that it could embark on its voyage overseas to be eaten by someone who doesn't even know whether cashews grow on trees or in the ground.

A seasoned critic might be impressed with the strong message of the drawing: the inadequate food, the painful labor, and the long hours. The same critic would probably also point out some of the technical flaws in the skyline of trees, the brown of the ground that had made its way onto the worn sleeves which concealed the arms in the foreground, or the discrepancies in the lengths of the fingers. These were easy mistakes for a six-year-old artist to make.

Chandra Sandeep had been only five years old when he lost his parents. His father had labored where he could to support his young family of four. His search for employment had often led him to the local cashew orchards, where he labored harvesting, sorting, and peeling the deliciously dangerous fruit. When opportunity and necessity presented themselves, the latter of which was always present, his lovely wife would join him in the work and, likewise, in the blisters and the lesions. Neither of them minded it much, though. It was a small price to pay for a solid roof over their heads and food in the bellies of the two jewels they called Kalini and Chandra.

Notwithstanding their perpetual state of indigence, they were a wonderfully happy family. When he wasn't working, which wasn't often, Chandra's father played incessantly with his two little ones. Chandra, being the youngest, got spoiled with the only thing his father could give: his time. One of his favorite games to play was "ride the elephant."

"Your Majesty," his father would say as Chandra would ascend to his throne upon his dad's slender but powerful back.

Chandra gave the command, "Forward." His father would then meander slowly through the house, and Chandra acted like royalty sitting upon a northern Indian howdah.

At the small table where they ate, Chandra would tap his scepter and say, "May good food bless this humble home."

Next, he would meet the commoners, such as his mother, whom he would kiss and bless. "Prosperity and beautiful children be with thee. One day your boy-child shall do great things."

Chandra giggled at the fun he had on his dad's back, but what was more memorable was what happened afterward. The game always wrapped up with some counsel from Abhijay to Chandra. "We make believe now, little Chandra, but one day you will have your opportunity to be great in this world. Your Appa knows it. You will get an education and never work a day in a cashew orchard. You are such a good boy. You must promise your Appa that you will stay a good boy all your life."

With all the confidence a five-year-old could muster, Chandra dutifully and anxiously always replied, "I promise, Appa," solemnizing the promise with a hug.

A smile and occasionally a tear would grace Abhijay's face as he responded hopefully, "I know you will. Appa looks forward to it."

Unfortunately, however, Appa never saw that day come. One horribly fateful day in Chandra's sixth year, his parents were traveling home by foot—the only way they traveled. From out of nowhere, they were hit by an unknown assailant driving a seldom-seen car—where they lived, only out-of-towners drove cars—much too fast for the dirt roads in the area they called home. Chandra's parents never came home that night, and even though intuition had given him the heads-up that Amma and Appa were not okay, it was two days before Chandra officially heard the life-shattering news. These were the first of several losses in young

Chandra's life. Certainly, he was as innocent as any other five-year-old boy, but even at that tender age, he felt he would hurt the person who drove that car if he were ever given the chance.

But young Chandra was quite unable to do anything about the situation. So, he confided in the only two things in life he felt he had: his sister and artwork. Kalini had been a good sister to Chandra for as long as he could remember. Of course she had teased him a little, and on an occasion or two had made him cry, but she loved her little brother, like most siblings do. But now that little Chandra had no family besides her, her young and precocious mind knew that she had to become more affectionate and loving towards her little brother. The moment they heard the news, they both started to cry, and Kalini, in terrible pain herself, buried her little brother's face in her chest so that he didn't have to cry alone.

Little Chandra looked up at his sister with teary eyes. "Why did the Americans kill Amma and Appa?"

Kalini wasn't sure what to say. It was such a big question for such a little person. She wanted to be strong for her brother and be the one he turned to, but how could she answer questions about things like death when she herself was but eight years old? She was uncomfortable as she started speaking. "Chandra, it was an accident. Nobody killed them."

Chandra explained, "Appa always told me that the rich American visitors drive the nice cars."

Kalini understood his point, but not wanting to dwell on her own pain, she tried to end the conversation. "Chandra, it was an accident. Nobody knows what happened."

"Except the person who killed them," replied Chandra abruptly.

"You don't know, and neither do I. But Amma and Appa are gone. We just have to remember the fun we always had at home." Then, Kalini put her little brother's head back into her chest and both of them started crying again. Thus started the beginning of an unbreakable relationship between two siblings orphaned at the young ages of five and eight.

Like most children, Chandra had some things that he wouldn't tell his parents or his sibling but still needed to hash out in his mind. Thus, when Kalini was not consoling him, Chandra turned to his artwork. His young and often bruised mind went to the canvas, or rather to the paper, to his world where he could journal things that even Kalini did not know or understand. What he saw, how he felt, and his plans for the future weren't really known to anyone, but they were drawn or painted symbolically when he had time and supplies, on a large notepad he had gotten as a present from his mom on his third birthday. The drawing of the plantation that hung in his room was his best work as a child. It was also his most emotion-filled piece thus far, and throughout his life, those sketches and paintings that came from his deepest emotions would be his masterpieces.

# CHAPTER 2

# CHANDRA'S GUARDIAN

---

**2007–2010 India**

Wealth and luxury were not part of the vocabulary that had existed in the Sandeep family, but the parents' hard work had made it possible to purchase the little shanty they called home. A strong work ethic, however, did not run in the Sandeep family. Chandra's father had an older brother, Navnit, who was not known for anything other than laziness and alcohol. Because Chandra's dad had his own place, Navnit considered him a rich man. Immediately after Chandra's parents died, the uncle took possession of the household and got just what he had always wanted: a free place to live. However, he also got what he'd never wanted: kids.

Chandra never forgot the first time he tried to play with his uncle. He smelled of cheap beer and could barely keep his eyes open as he turned his head to speak. "Can't you see I'm busy? Go play with your sister." Then he shut his eyes and fell asleep. That short episode epitomized the whole of Chandra's interactions with his uncle. He never took his niece or nephew anywhere, he never played with them, and he only occasionally fed them. Lucky for Chandra, he was not alone.

His sister, still not yet nine years old, could see the disappointment in her little brother's eyes. She got down on all fours and beckoned to her brother, "Your Majesty."

Chandra hesitated at first—it definitely wasn't going to be the same as riding daddy's strong back—but Kalini made the best elephant noises she could muster, and his royal majesty ascended to his portable throne.

Kalini flinched from the weight of someone not much lighter than she. "Are you okay?" Chandra asked, about to jump off. Kalini simply answered by trumpeting. Then, pachyderm style, she conducted Prince Chandra around his kingdom to check on matters of royalty and to lift her little brother's spirits. This happened several times for the next year, and Chandra remembered it for the rest of his life.

Just three short years later, even in Chandra's prepubescent mind, he understood that his sister, for all intents and purposes, was running the family. Their uncle's new parental responsibilities had made no impact on his work ethic. So, there were one hungry adult and two hungry children to feed. Nervous but unshrinking, his sister had entered the workforce. As soon as Chandra was old enough to understand what was going on, he too found employment, and between the two of them they could make ends meet and feed their useless uncle.

Although Chandra grew out of riding the elephant, he and Kalini played together as often as they could, but it was not always easy to find time. Unlike many of the more well-to-do kids, they went to school during the day and worked in the evenings. Chandra hardly made a rupee, but Kalini was able to earn a meaningful amount of money at the market working for a farmer who had known their parents.

Kalini managed all the money they made. She gave a portion of her earnings directly to her uncle but wisely hid the rest to ensure that, despite their "guardian's" dereliction of familial duty, Chandra would not go hungry. What Chandra didn't realize until later was that this did not always mean that his wonderful sister did not go hungry.

On a smoldering hot day in Chandra's eleventh year, his sister had come home from the market where she had earned what little she could. Chandra's mouth was watering as he helped her make a modest dal, and they had some naan to go with it. Their uncle took the lion's share—far more than Kalini had hoped he would take. Not taking too much notice because of his own excessive hunger, Chandra scraped up some of the delicious golden dal with his naan. Unfortunately, there really wasn't much left after his uncle had taken his whopping portion and gone back to sleep. The growling in Chandra's stomach—audible to Kalini—publicized his want for more dinner. All that was left for poor Kalini were two meager pieces of naan—the only food she would have the whole day. Chandra dared not ask for more, knowing that his sister had spent the day working. Kalini, on the other hand, had enough motherly intuition to know why her little brother's eyes were so big. So, hiding her exhaustion and hunger, she faked a smile and lied. "I ate at the market, and I'm really not that hungry. Do you want my bread?" Even with the smile on her face and the joy of helping her little brother, it hurt to say those words.

Happy but hesitant, Chandra replied, "Are you sure?"

Content on the outside but crying inside, she said, "I really just need to get to my summer assignment. I'm not that hungry."

Chandra took the naan and gladly ate it while Kalini went to the candle with her books and pretended to work on an assignment she didn't have. Seeing her focused on her supposed studies, Chandra went to bed. However, about an hour later, something woke him. At first he thought it was his uncle snoring and talking in his sleep—sounds he was accustomed to hearing throughout the day—but it wasn't. He heard whimpering. He looked up, and there he saw his sister, still sitting by the candle, head in her hands, sobbing. Though he was only eleven turning twelve, Chandra knew what had happened. He understood the sacrifice that his sister had made. He loved her all the more for it, but he was heartbroken and ashamed of what he had done. Painfully full of remorse and not knowing how to apologize, he slowly got up, went to his sister and embraced her. Embarrassed that she had been seen crying and not quite sure how to respond, Kalini hugged him back amid sobs. Uncharacteristic of most young boys, Chandra told his sister he loved her. Kalini smiled wanly, kissed his forehead, and told him to go to sleep.

Chandra obeyed, but he kept a watchful eye on his sister. She gathered her things and went to bed as well. Chandra hadn't gone to bed on a completely empty stomach, so he did not really know what that would feel like. He had, however, gone to bed a little hungry and did know what that felt like: a constant pull in the pit of your belly and a headache reminding you that you need more food. Every time he saw his sister toss or turn in the night, he knew what her body was telling her, and he knew that the hunger pangs she was experiencing were likely far stronger than anything he had experienced.

As he lay in bed, he wondered how often this had happened. His mind raced back through the past three years. Tonight was definitely not the first time. Nor was it the second, third, fourth, fifth... Chandra felt sick to his stomach that he had taken his sister's food so many times. And anytime it wasn't a school day, she probably had spent the whole day fasting.

And though this had happened more times than Chandra could or even wanted to count, he never remembered Kalini ever complaining for a moment. Chandra's eleven-year-old emotions started to swell. How he loved his sister. She was indeed more than a sister. The sacrifices of her time, her money, and even her food had gone unnoticed by Chandra, but they all were coming into full view now.

Then it hit him. She had carried him on her back when he was young. She was providing for the family. She even told him when it was time for bed. Yes, she was more than a sister. Kalini was essentially his mom and had been for half of his life.

Lying there on his mat bed, Chandra decided that he would no longer treat Kalini as he had. Certainly, he had loved her and would have done what he could for her, but now it was different. Now that he realized she was his mother, he would act more like a son. Part of that would be not eating all the food until he was sure that she had eaten. More than that though, he would support her, he would work harder to try to earn a little more, he would make sure she could achieve some of her own goals, and most importantly he would keep her safe from the predators he saw all around them.

# CHAPTER 3

# From Bullied to Bully

**2010–2015 India**

About a kilometer and a half away, just on the outskirts of town, was an American-sponsored Catholic school. Generally speaking, it was filled with students of two varieties: the vast majority were Indian children from well-to-do families, and the rest were foreign students whose parents worked either at the school or in the area through a variety of relief and charity organizations. Needless to say, the Sandeep children did not exactly fit the mold, but through Kalini's hard work and wisdom, they were able to pay some tuition, which was extremely low, and get scholarships for the bulk of their expenses.

However, being in a nice school did not equate to always being around nice people. To be certain, most of the students were very good, well-mannered kids. However, over the years there were a few American children of businesspeople who had not had the same upbringing as their mission service counterparts. Rather than embrace the culture of the Southern Indian people, quite to the contrary, they created a culture of bullying. These children were few in number but unfortunately popular, and their influence oozed onto others around them, even other Indian children.

This did not bode well for Chandra. There were two things that these American boys, along with their rich Indian friends, looked for in prey: scrawniness and indigence. Chandra's home situation made for a double whammy and put him on the top of the hit list.

His fears became reality early in his sixth year of school, when he committed the damnable sin of using the restroom. Unfortunately for him, four other boys full of mischief followed him. They had with them a large bowl that they had filled with precious water some other students had worked hard to fetch. While Chandra was attempting to defecate, they burst in and dumped the water all over poor Chandra, pointing fingers of ridicule at him and laughing, then ran out of the lavatory, victorious.

Chandra felt ashamed. About a quarter of the class—including the boys, one an American, who had done the dastardly deed—laughed at him scornfully when he came into the room. The rest of the class did not find it funny, but Chandra didn't look to see who was or was not laughing. He just put his head down on the desk and told the teacher he'd not been careful. It was the last time that he used the restroom until his junior year, by which time he was much larger and, when necessary, much more aggressive.

When Chandra was thirteen, there was another ill-tempered American kid in the school. Chandra had accidentally bumped into the kid as he was running out of the classroom on his way to play. The American boy had had a seldom-seen Coca Cola in his hand, and some of it spilled onto his shirt and pants. The kid was livid.

The boy and four of his friends threw Chandra against the hallway wall before he had a chance to get away. The boy yelled in Chandra's face, "You're gonna pay for this, you..." He added some other choice words in English that Chandra was only partially able to understand, but even without knowing what they meant, he could tell the boy was not asking if he wanted to play soccer in the courtyard.

"I'm sorry!" he yelled back desperately, but his words had no effect. Chandra thought he was going to get the beating of a lifetime. Just as the boys were about to pummel him, someone yelled out with enough authority to get everyone's attention, "Stop!"

Sure enough it was Kalini. Kalini wasn't a very large person, but she could be commanding when needed. She also had something else that made her quite imposing, especially to young boys: Kalini was gorgeous. Now sixteen, she was by far the most beautiful girl in the school, and there had already been a few middle-income men who had tried unsuccessfully to court her. So, stunned by her demand and her good looks, the boys ran away.

Shaken but coherent, Chandra said, "Still looking after me, huh?"

Kalini understood well what he meant but feigned ignorance. "What do you mean?"

Chandra smirked. "I think you know." He picked up the things he had dropped while trying to defend himself and said, "You've always taken care of me."

A guy walked by trying to catch Kalini's eye, but she took no notice. "Well, what do you expect? I am your older sister," she said, ruffling his hair.

"Right," said Chandra, thinking, *More like my mom.* "I just wish the Americans would stay away."

Kalini's motherly wisdom told her what he was thinking, but she wanted him to say it anyway. "What's wrong with Americans, Chandra?"

"They are always causing problems."

Kalini kept a smile on her face. "You know that's not true. We've known a lot of kids who are here because their parents are out here serving people like you and me. You can't think they're all bad."

Chandra wanted to respect his sister while still making his point. "There may be *some* good ones, but all I know is that every time I get picked on, it's because some American is up to no good."

Kalini had to admit there usually was a white kid in the posse when Chandra was bullied, but she did not want him stereotyping all Americans the same way. "I've had a couple American friends. They were nice."

"Maybe they were just nice to you because you're popular."

Kalini chuckled.

Not really expecting much of a response from Kalini, Chandra said, "I personally think India would be better off without them."

Kalini stopped him right there. "Chandra, I don't want you saying things like this. You said I have tried to take care of you? Well, here is something I want you to listen to. Perhaps you have had some trouble with Americans, but I promise that if you look you will find plenty of good Americans. And if you let yourself think things like you just said, you are only going to get yourself into trouble."

Chandra took a chance at defiance and tried to persuade his sister with something that was sure to pull on her heartstrings. "Kalini, Americans killed Mom and Dad."

"Stop!" Kalini said with as much vigor as she'd used on the group of boys a minute before. Her eyes started to tear up. "I know Amma and Appa are gone. Thank you for the reminder." Her lower lip quivered. "I also know that we have no idea what happened, and even if it was an American; you can't live your life villainizing others because of a few bad people." She stopped talking so that she would not lose her composure and kept walking towards home.

Chandra was embarrassed. Though he agreed to drop the subject, he still didn't feel any different about Americans, but that wasn't the cause of his shame. He was ashamed because he had hurt his sister. How could he hurt the only person in the world who meant anything to him? Regardless of how he felt about Americans, he wasn't going to let his anger affect his sister. If he were to hurt her... he couldn't think about it. She meant the world to him.

Nonetheless, time has a funny way of helping people forget their resolutions, and Chandra was no exception. Gradually, he only became more jaded towards Americans. The bullying, however, came to an abrupt stop in his fifteenth year.

It happened early on a very ordinary day in the hallway. An American and a couple of Indian boys were standing next to the wall. As he walked by, he didn't pay them any attention, and the American boy stuck his foot out to trip him. Though Chandra didn't fall, he did stumble and drop his things on the floor. It was almost instinctive: he looked down at his papers strewn all over the dirty wood panels, and, in one motion, he screamed and nailed the American right on the nose with his fist. The American boy immediately cowered as blood started running from his nostrils, covering his lips and hand. Then he and the two other boys raced to the bathroom.

Chandra was stunned, but not because he had punched someone or because they ran. He was stunned that he felt exhilarated. The emotions that surged over him as he struck someone, the excitement of seeing the boy's face contort in agony, and the shock and thrill of seeing blood, a sure sign of damage, filled him with an awesome sense of power. It was an invigoration that he would not pass up again and one that kept him safe from being bullied. Unfortunately, the poor scrawny boy who had once been bullied now became a bully.

During the second half of the year, a Canadian boy moved in for a few months. His dad was working throughout the area installing wells through a charity called River of Life. This sweet young man was enjoying a friendly conversation with a group of six Indian kids. He was explaining how back home he had built a ramp with his friends so that they could jump their bikes. Unfortunately, the ramp had broken when it was his turn to jump, and he'd been flung right over the handlebars headlong onto the ground. "I was like, *'Aahhhhhh!'*" he said, making everyone laugh.

Chandra had just come out of a room at the same moment and thought it was another dumb American making fun of him. So, without thinking, he came up behind the boy and shoved him out of the way, making him hit his head against that of one of his friends.

A girl spoke up, "Stop, you jerk."

Chandra just brushed it off. *Stupid American rubbish,* he thought.

Kalini, who had been waiting to walk him home, saw the whole thing transpire. She knew that Chandra was becoming more and more hostile towards Americans, which, in his mind, virtually all Caucasians were. She felt sad. What more could she do to help Chandra let go of his anger? She had to confront him about it. She doubted that it would help, but, like any good mother, or sister, she did not avoid the topic.

"Chandra, did that boy do something to you?"

It had become so second-nature for Chandra to act like that towards others that he sincerely did not know what she was talking about. "What boy?"

Kalini shot him a disapproving, incredulous look, "The boy you just shoved."

"He was making fun of me."

Kalini knew he did not know what the boy had said. "Making fun of you?" she said. "What did he say?"

Chandra just kept calmly walking towards home, not really paying attention to what Kalini was saying. "I don't know."

In an effort to get her brother to at least attempt to think about what they were discussing, Kalini pried further. "Then how do you know that he said anything about you at all?"

Chandra shrugged his shoulders, not really caring what the boy had said and not really wanting to have the conversation. "They always do."

Trying to fight the generalizations, Kalini dug a little deeper to lead Chandra to discover his own folly. "What do you mean, *they*?"

Chandra did not like to disrespect his sister, but he was irritated, and he snapped back. "The Americans! They are always trying to make my life miserable."

Kalini sighed to herself. Could anything she say help? They had had this conversation before. Why did he refuse to see what she and every other kid in the school saw? If he wasn't going to come to the right conclusions about the world and people on his own, she was going to have to force that view upon him. She cared too much for her little brother to allow him to continue on a path that would lead him to who knows where. She had to give it a shot. "Chandra. I love you. You know that, right?"

Chandra was confused and gave her a very slow, "Yeeessss..."

"Then you've got to trust me. First of all, not all white kids, including the one you just pushed, are Americans. And second, I promise you, not all Americans are bad, and I need you to promise me that you will not start another fight because of the color of someone's skin."

Chandra kept walking. Though Kalini had been like a mother to him, he was an adolescent, and he was starting to lose respect for her. He just shrugged his shoulders again and said, "Sure."

Kalini pushed harder, "Promise me."

Offhanded, he said, "I promise."

Kalini knew he was barely even paying attention. She stopped directly in front of him and said, "Look me in the eyes."

He obeyed.

Now that their eyes were locked, he felt uncomfortable. Her eyes were so intense. These were the eyes of not only the one person he loved, but the only person on the planet who loved him. Her eyes brought in a flood of memories of all she had sacrificed for him. He could not look into her eyes and lie.

Kalini had all of her emotions on the table for Chandra to see: disappointment, fear, concern. She needed him to stop because she hated to think of the road that her little brother was on. Where would it lead?

Unemployment? Abuse? Jail? Death? She couldn't, she wouldn't hold back, and a tear fell down her face as she stared at him eye to eye.

"Promise me right now that you will not start another fight with an American."

Chandra wavered. "Kalini…"

She stopped him, even more stern. "Promise me, right now!"

He tried to say something else. "B—"

"Promise me."

Love overcame defiance. He hugged his mother–sister–best friend. "I promise." And Chandra was faithful to his word, even though it soon came at odds with his determination to protect his sister.

# CHAPTER 4

# Keeping His Promise

---

**2015–2016 India**

Midway through the same year, which was Kalini's last year of school, Chandra watched two things unfold that brought him much grief and tested his commitment to not harass Americans. It was as if the fates were against him and the worst possible things that could happen were happening.

First, a few months into the school year, his sister got a new job. This was not a problem in and of itself, but Chandra did not like her boss. His name was George Smith.

Though Chandra's jaded eyes were far too blind to see it, Dr. Smith was a good man. He had left America immediately after graduating from medical school at the young age of twenty-five. Being at the top of his class, he could have gotten a job wherever he fancied, but that was never his intention. After doing a one-year internship in internal medicine, he joined Doctors Without Borders, and after a year and a half in India, he decided to make the country his home.

Dr. Smith was the secretary, nurse, and attending physician at his practice, which mostly served the poorest of the poor. Even so, he made enough money to hire a desperately needed assistant. When Kalini showed up, she was an answer to a prayer. She did not require much money, she had no qualms about cleaning the clinic, she was happy to do the secretarial administration, and was more than happy to interpret for Dr. Smith and his patients when his Tamil, progressing but still nascent, was insufficient.

Chandra distrusted the young doctor around his sister. Chandra was not blind to his sister's beauty. Over the past couple years, he had seen his sister approached by women clad in fine apparel trying to recruit her into the devilish industry of prostitution, which was pervasive in their city. The women were lovely and tried to convince Kalini that she could escape the hell she lived in for freedom with a high-paying clientele, but Kalini knew hell when she saw it and never acquiesced.

Chandra once asked what had happened after seeing such an encounter, but Kalini just brushed it off as someone looking for directions. Chandra, however, was not so naive and knew exactly what had transpired.

And so, a little more money in their pockets from her job at the doctor's office was nice, but Chandra wanted to make sure that Kalini was not getting any unsolicited anatomy lessons. And considering his previous interactions with Americans, he would not have trusted Dr. Smith even if he were thirty years his sister's senior. With only ten years between the two, he would need to be even more vigilant.

Chandra's second problem was a new kid at school, named T.J. Banks. He was a senior, but this was his first year both at the school and in India. Chandra didn't notice, but almost every girl in the school noticed how much like iconic David of old, he was quite a work of art. His six-foot-tall frame carried little soft fat and a fair amount of hard muscle. Among a sea of students' short dark hair, his blond waves easily caught the eye, and his penetrating blue eyes were like a husky's in the middle of winter. His teeth were exquisitely white, as only whitening strips can make them, and were strikingly offset by the tan that he had achieved through weeks, if not months, of spraying.

T.J. was from a well-to-do family. His father was an up-and-coming executive for Dyya Beetees, a sugar company. The company grew sugar beets and had just acquired a medium-sized sugar cane company in India to expand their portfolio. His father had been put in charge of integrating the newly acquired business.

In preparation for the move, T.J.'s parents had hired a private tutor for him, and before he even arrived in India, he could hold a conversation in Tamil. After a mere three months in the country, he could speak well enough that he seldom was confused in a one-on-one conversation, and after five months he could understand almost every conversation around him.

Indeed, T.J. was something special, and after a while, even level-headed Kalini took notice. Unfortunately, T.J. took notice of her as well.

On an otherwise normal day, Chandra saw Kalini sitting down to eat lunch at school. This was quite an oddity. Because of her busy schedule, she never ate lunch at school; she just grabbed something on her way to work at the clinic. Chandra sat beside her. He had no malign intentions, but Kalini knew that, in the end, Chandra was going to be upset at her being there.

With a smile on his face, Chandra asked, "Hey, sis, what are you doing here?"

Kalini, pretending that everything was normal, responded playfully, "What, can't I eat lunch, too?"

Chandra laughed back and responded, "Yeah, but you never do."

Kalini smiled. "Well, I guess there is a first time for everything."

He chuckled at her comment but didn't think too much of it. His smile quickly went away with what happened next.

A white kid came and sat across from them at the table. He wore a huge smile, one that Chandra could see right through. Chandra did not like that this boy was sitting near them, but he loved his sister more and kept his promise to her not to overreact.

"Hi, Kalini, is this your brother?"

*She's friends with him?* thought Chandra. *Why?*

"Yes, this is Chandra, my brother," replied Kalini, giving Chandra a smile and a squeeze. Chandra didn't smile back. Kalini continued, "Chandra, T.J. T.J., Chandra."

"Nice to meet you," replied T.J., and without waiting for a response, he turned to Kalini. "You look nice today."

Kalini blushed but internally flinched as she knew Chandra was getting angry.

Then T.J. asked: "So are you good for Friday night?"

*Friday night?* thought Chandra. *What does he care about her Friday night?* Chandra started going through a mental calendar. What was on Friday night? No school functions. No festivals. Nothing is going on. Unless...

"I am free. I'll see you there," responded Kalini.

*She's going on a date with this guy? She must be out of her mind*, thought Chandra. *There are half a billion boys in India. Why is she going out with this stupid American?*

"Are you sure? My dad has a nice car. We could pick you up."

*Why am I not surprised*, fumed Chandra. *First the Americans kill my mom and dad; now they are after my sister. This moron is going to be the death of my sister. I know it.* Chandra couldn't help himself; he spoke up, "I will go with her."

Disappointed but not showing it, T.J. asked. "Okay, you want to come, too?"

Though she appreciated his concern, Kalini wasn't going to let her little brother run her life. "Chandra, thank you for offering to walk me, but I will be fine walking to the restaurant, and T.J. is more than capable of walking me back home." She turned to T.J. "Is that okay?"

Relieved, T.J. responded, "Sure!" and before things could get stranger, he said his goodbyes and left the table.

Chandra looked at Kalini in disbelief. "What are you doing? Why would you go out with him?"

"Chandra, when was the last time that you saw me go out to have fun?" asked Kalini.

Chandra knew what she was getting at, but why this guy? Why now? "I don't know."

Matter-of-factly, she interrogated him a little further, "Try to guess."

"I don't know."

"You don't know because it doesn't happen. I have only been able to spend time with my girlfriends a few times a year, and I have only ever gone on one date. I want to get out."

Chandra didn't really know what to say. He knew that she was right but didn't like the idea anyway. "Why him?"

"He seems like a nice guy." Kalini decided not to tell Chandra that she had turned T.J. down a few times in the past.

"Are you in love?"

Chandra did not know it, but that was a hard question for Kalini. She definitely was not in love with T.J., but there was someone else who was often on her mind. But how could he love her? She was just a poor young girl, not yet out of high school. He was a successful man ten years her senior. She wasn't sure if it was love, but she had strong feelings for her boss. It wasn't something that she was going to bring up with him, let alone with Chandra, and after a brief pause she came back to the conversation and focused on T.J.

"Of course not. I barely even know him." She paused and looked her brother directly in the eyes. "Chandra, I am going out with T.J., whether you like it or not—"

Chandra cut her off. "I don't like it."

"It doesn't matter. You can walk me there if you want, but you won't be staying, and you won't be walking me home. Do you understand?"

Chandra hated it, but he couldn't talk back to the only parental figure he had. "I understand," he mumbled. He understood he had lost this fight, but if anything happened to Kalini, he would be repaying the deed.

# CHAPTER 5

# Kalini's Hot Date

**2016 India**

Other than getting home a little later than she had said, it appeared to Chandra that the date went as he had hoped. It was a one-time event. Without giving any details, Kalini just told her brother that she was uninterested in T.J. It was the truth.

A few days later, Chandra saw a small cut and a bruise on his sister's wrist. Without hesitation, Kalini explained what happened. She told him that at the clinic she had scraped her arm on a door while trying to help an elderly woman into her room. Chandra accepted this answer and was relieved to hear that no one had hurt her. Kalini was relieved, too. It was a lie.

Turned out T.J. was not a good boy.

During dinner it had only taken a few minutes for her to realize that T.J. had one thing on his mind. And poor Kalini also had one thing on her mind. She had only been to a restaurant a few times in her life. Most of the occasions were recent and with Dr. Smith. But, alas, they were only lunches for business. The whole time she was there with T.J., she was wishing she were with Dr. Smith instead.

As they walked home, though she didn't like it, she allowed T.J. to hold her hand. Doing so made her feel horribly uncomfortable, even betrayed somehow. Or maybe she felt like she was betraying someone else. She had felt so many emotions through the evening that she felt sick. Even if she were not betraying a man who loved her, she was at the very least betraying her own heart. She tried to get away by mentioning she was cold and folding her arms, but that only made matters worse. Now he had his arm around her.

With each step T.J. was trying to figure out what his next move should be. Should he kiss her? Should he ask her on another date? She didn't seem to mind him holding her as they walked. Maybe a couple of intimate kisses and touches would get her more interested.

As they approached the shanty she called home, T.J. gave Kalini a few kisses on the neck. She tried to pull back but was interrupted by a grab on her left butt cheek. She had had enough!

"What are you doing?" she demanded.

"I'm just trying to give you the attention you deserve," T.J. responded as he bent down to get a better taste of her skin.

"This is more attention than I ever want from you."

Even with a good education, T.J. had somehow picked up the virulent infection of racism during his youth. Being in India among people who were less fortunate than him, at least from a monetary standpoint, had only exacerbated the problem. He was not about to be rejected or spoken to like that by someone who, in his mind, was inferior: a poor orphan girl. His tone abruptly changed from seductive to derogatory. "Well, I paid for dinner. Is this how you say thanks?"

Kalini noticed the sudden change and, turning away, said, "I'm leaving."

"What's the problem?" said T.J. as he grabbed her wrist.

"I don't want to be treated this way."

"Treated what way? You're the one being rude to me."

"I want to leave."

"Kalini, stop. I'm sorry," he said, trying to act sorrowful but deep down trying to get a little action.

"I'm sorry, too," she replied, momentarily softening T.J.'s mood. "I'm sorry I ever agreed to this date. Good night."

"Why are you being so rude? I have been nothing but nice to you ever since I met you."

"All you have tried to do is kiss me, or touch me, or whatever else. Well, it's not going to happen. I am going home to my family, and if I need to yell to get their attention, I will."

"Well, you've got me wrong, and if that's how you are going to act, then you'd better keep an eye out for your family. I wouldn't want anything bad to happen to your little brother."

Kalini sensed that she was in danger. As she yanked her arm from his hand, his fingernail cut her, and she took off running. T.J. would have gone after her and tried one more time to get her to acquiesce, but they were too close to the house. He had a better idea anyway. So, rejected, he started thinking of how he could bring his idea to life and headed back to his house.

Kalini ran home, then allowed herself to catch her breath before going inside. She acted as though nothing had happened, knowing that if Chandra found out, it would only anger him more against Americans and perhaps lead to his ruin. And so, with her little lie of omission, Chandra's anger was kept at bay, but that, too, did not last for long.

# CHAPTER 6

# LOVE

---

**April 2016 India**

There were few places to hide anything in the Sandeep home. Their shanty consisted of a place to cook, a place to eat, and a place to sleep; that was it. There was one bookcase, but other than that, if something was to be kept, it was kept on the floor near one's bed.

Though Kalini had said she had no interest in T.J., since the time of their date, Chandra, who regularly tidied the house while his sister worked, kept an eye out for any signs of love between the two. Thankfully there was none, and all casual conversations with his sister led to the same conclusion: Chandra did not have to worry about an American brother-in-law, or so he thought.

Since Kalini was getting close to graduating, Chandra was accustomed to seeing papers for school admissions near her bed. Less occasionally, he caught glimpses of postings for jobs in the city. It would be hard for him to be without his sister. Chandra still did not have any true friends, and being without Kalini would basically mean being without family as well. Nonetheless, he wanted to support his sole protector in childhood and the only person on earth who had helped him understand what it meant to feel love.

While cleaning one day, Chandra encountered something that brought him no small amount of heartache, disappointment, and most poignantly, anger.

Kalini was mostly careful not to show or talk to Chandra about things that would upset him. After all, as far as she could tell, Chandra had been true to his word about not fighting with Americans. Still, she did not want him knowing certain things—at least not until she was completely ready to tell him.

But, as careful as she was, on one occasion she let her guard down.

Chandra was sweeping the floor and tossing away beer bottles strewn about by Navnit. As he made the normal rounds through the house, he saw a card on Kalini's pillow. It wasn't Kalini's writing. The writing style was sloppy, as if a child had written it.

At a quick glance, he saw the word *love* scribbled on it. *That's cute,* he thought, immediately assuming some young boy at the clinic had been struck with his sister's charm and wrote her a secret love note. Seeing no harm, he picked up the card.

It wasn't from a little kid. Chandra's heart was broken. It was from someone who had poor penmanship, both in his native language and in Tamil.

Chandra felt sick to his stomach as he read the words.

Kalini,

I know you have a lot on your mind these days with decisions about school and work. Because of that, there are a couple of things I thought would be easier for me to write than to say.

I was not surprised to hear that you were accepted to very prestigious schools in England and here in India. I am sure no matter where you go, you will excel.

You have been a wonderful help here at the clinic and you are welcome to stay as long as you please, but I know that you are capable of great things and perhaps you don't want to be at a small clinic in a small town.

If you go away for school or a better job, I will pay you for the next month to make sure you are okay and will recommend you to any doctor in India or around the world.

Kalini, I will support whatever decision you make, but I need you to know that if you leave, my world will shatter. The thought of never seeing you again is too much for my heart to take. I love you.

George

*I never trusted him,* thought Chandra. How would he approach this? It was crazy. She was barely eighteen. Could Kalini fall for someone ten years older than her? Or was he already taking advantage of her and had been for some time?

Where was Kalini now? She wasn't terribly late, but she should have been home already. Chandra had terrible thoughts of what an adult American might be doing with his teenage, barely adult sister. If someone hurt his sister, he didn't know what he would do, but justice would be served.

For the next hour, the roles of Chandra and Kalini changed. Normally she was worried where her brother was, or whether something had happened to him, or if he was okay at school. Now it was the opposite. Like the father of a teenage girl, patient but extremely worried, Chandra waited for his sister. When she finally got home, he expected she would be acting differently than usual. But no. It was like any other day. She did not let on that anything had happened, and she immediately went about her normal routine. Chandra started to wonder how long she had been hiding something.

"Thanks for cleaning up, Chandra. I brought home a couple of small dosa. I can make something to go with them if you like," she said.

Confused, Chandra mused whether she had even seen the card. But how could she not have seen it? It was on her pillow. He was definitely going to bring it up, but he hoped that she would first. "The dosa is fine. I can take the smaller one so you can eat."

"Oh, I'm not hungry," said Kalini as she started to clean up the things that Chandra had overlooked.

"I have heard you say that before, and I'm not going to let you go hungry again," said Chandra, hoping to get a little more information as to why she was not hungry and why she had brought home the dosa in the first place.

"I already ate. I'm really not hungry. You don't need to worry," said Kalini playfully, ruffling his hair.

"How was work?" Chandra asked, trying to sound innocent.

"Fine," Kalini responded with little interest but a bit of deception.

"How is Dr. Smith?" Chandra inquired further.

Now Kalini started to worry. Chandra never asked about Dr. Smith. Still, she still feigned normalcy, "He's fine."

Chandra was impatient. He had to protect his sister. He pulled out the card. "What is this all about?"

Kalini was not happy that her brother had read such a personal note. "Where did you get that?" she demanded.

Chandra saw her displeasure but knew he was acting in her best interest, so he answered, "I saw it—"

Kalini cut him off. "On my bed. Where you should not have been snooping."

"I'm just trying to help you—"

Kalini cut him off again. "Help me? By looking through my things? How is that helping me?"

"Kalini, I can't let you get involved with some American..."

"Can't let me? Chandra, you don't make decisions for me. I can do what I want."

"He'll destroy your life."

Kalini could not believe what was coming out of her little brother's mouth. Chandra had no idea what he was talking about, nor how much Dr. Smith had done for him. "Chandra, have you noticed that we haven't been as hungry as we used to be?"

"I don't know, maybe," he said, feeling that the conversation was quickly getting out of his control.

"That's because when Dr. Smith found out what our home life was like, he started paying me more."

Chandra was a very smart young man, but being upset, he took her comment at face value. Seeing an opportunity to expose Dr. Smith, Chandra found this comment helpful to his argument.

"He is using you. He is paying you more to win you over so that he can use you for what he wants; then he'll get rid of you. You're having sex with him, aren't you?"

If Kalini could not believe what Chandra was saying before, she was now flabbergasted by this inquiry. Her brother—her younger brother, the one she had cared for all his life—was trying to scold her. Unlike Chandra, she was not taking things at face value in her moment of anger. She understood why Chandra was upset. She understood that Chandra wanted to help, but she couldn't be flattered. None of that mattered. She was in charge of the household, and Chandra's racism had blinded his judgment. As she began to respond, her face reflected a calm indignation that commanded both attention and obedience. "Chandra, I am eighteen years old. I can do with my life as I choose. It is none of your business what I do in my personal time. Do you understand that?"

"I just want to know if he is taking advantage of you."

"I will determine who is taking advantage of who, but you are to keep out of my personal life. Do I make myself clear?"

Her uncompromising, severe expression caused Chandra no small amount of discomfort. Nonetheless, he did not feel ready to give up. "You didn't really answer my questions."

As straight-faced as ever, she inclined her head a little closer. "I do not need to answer your questions. But I will say this. I love Dr. Smith, and I will do all I can to make him happy. And just so you know, he is paying me more because he wants to make sure that the little brother I take care of does not need to go to bed hungry, the way I have in the past. This is the end of this conversation." At this, she turned away, still steaming, and resumed tidying the house.

Chandra was defeated on all fronts. *How could this have happened?* he thought. His sister in love—in a sexual relationship no less—with an American! His enemy. Their enemy. *How could she do this to me?* At the same time, he trusted his sister. Chandra was getting a headache. *Is it really possible that he is trying to take care of me?* Chandra did not like the idea of being nurtured by an American. *How could he even be capable of such a thing?*

With these thoughts whirling through his head, Chandra went to his bed to lie down. Then Kalini came to him again. "By the way, Dr. Smith and I will be married at the end of the school year. I hope you come, but I am not going to force you."

Bewildered, Chandra thought, *Could this day get any worse?* He didn't like it, but he would obviously need to support his sister. Unlike many other Indian weddings, there would be no big extended family in attendance. If Chandra didn't go, she would have no family there at all. He couldn't abandon her. The idea of a good American still made him uncomfortable. But his love for his sister was greater. Perhaps he could make an exception. *There are three hundred million people in America. Maybe Dr. Smith is okay.*

Chandra had to do something, because losing his sister was not an option. So, before he fell asleep, he made an internal commitment, one for Kalini. He promised himself that as long as Dr. Smith proved himself to be genuine, he would suffer him for Kalini's sake. So far, he had kept his promise to Kalini about fighting. He was not sure, however, that he could keep a promise made to himself.

# CHAPTER 7

# A Fight to Remember

---

**June 2016 India**

The school year had ended; Chandra had been true to his word to Kalini and to himself. It had been about a year since he had gotten into any fights, and he had been respectful to Dr. Smith, who had shown himself to be trustworthy. Kalini had graduated at the top of her class, and she was working full time. She and Dr. Smith had become open about their love, and her normally plain attire now had one flashy accessory: a ring.

Because she was working at the office, they could see each other throughout the day. So long as Dr. Smith wasn't staying late to take care of someone after hours, they had dinner together every night. Furthermore, Dr. Smith had given Kalini full assurance that she need not worry about Chandra. Together, they would support him financially, or Chandra would be welcome to live with them if he so chose. The years of hard work were finally starting to pay off for Kalini, but as often happens in life, some dreams just aren't meant to be.

Their woes started on a late afternoon in mid-June. No one had heard anything from or of T.J. in about a month. As far as Kalini was aware, he was assumed to have already departed for the US, but T.J. had some unfinished business.

Chandra was now working at Dr. Smith's office, and on this particular day he had finished sweeping the floor, a job that Kalini used to do, and was ready to go home. Kalini wasn't quite ready, but Chandra didn't want to wait. So, he set off about an hour before dusk to take the road home, the same one he had traveled for years from school.

Though warm by most standards, it was a rather cool Southern Indian June afternoon as Chandra made his way. As he passed the Indian Mahoganies and the curry trees, he was struggling inside. He was questioning his views of the world. He wasn't ready to go so far as to say that he liked an American, but he questioned his disdain. Perhaps other people weren't as bad as he thought.

His sister was about to marry an American, and Chandra could not find any reason to dislike the guy. After he had made his internal commitment to put up with Dr. Smith, he found Dr. Smith to be a good person. He felt confident that Dr. Smith would take care of his sister. *Was Dr. Smith the only American who was good?* His thoughts were complicated as he walked and mused on the issue. He could feel himself getting soft. He considered allowing a change of heart, but the feeling was abruptly interrupted.

Chandra heard some rustling behind a shrub. Before he could position himself for defense, a few unfamiliar Indian boys had grabbed both of his arms. T.J. then slowly approached him. Chandra knew what was going to happen next. Obviously, Dr. Smith was the only worthwhile American. His suppressed rage came flooding back in full force.

Chandra wriggled his body to make quick plans. He could tell that the boy on his right was not as strong as the one on his left. In an attempt to get them to loosen their grips, Chandra gritted his teeth and stopped moving.

T.J. had a smirk on his face and regarded Chandra disdainfully as a lesser creature. Looking at Chandra was both difficult and enraging. He looked too much like his sister for T.J. not to be reminded of her.

She was the first girl to reject him and the one whom he had wanted the most. The feelings of rejection shot through with sadness made the task at hand difficult. Yet the way she'd so bluntly rejected him, after he had been so good to her, was fuel to keep going.

As he walked toward Chandra, he said, "Your sister could have been a lucky girl."

Chandra ripped his right arm free and swung at T.J. He didn't quite reach so he continued his motion towards the boy on his left. Startled, T.J. punched Chandra in the torso, causing Chandra to retract his own punch. Suddenly Chandra was back to being held by both arms. He started to kick his captors and landed a couple of heels to their shins.

T.J. was not really sure what to do next. He had supposed that he could easily scare Chandra and rough him up a little, but he had a lot more on his hands than he had anticipated, and if he didn't act fast Chandra might get the better of him. He punched Chandra in the stomach two more times, but it seemed to have little effect, so he went for his face. It was the first time T.J. had ever punched anyone in the face, and frankly he didn't like doing it, but he felt now he was more defending himself than bullying. Chandra's lip started to bleed. The boys holding him were getting tired, but they gripped tighter as Chandra thrashed harder. T.J. swung from the side and squarely hit Chandra on the cheekbone. This slowed Chandra down.

T.J. had just raised his arm for one last blow to the face when he felt someone grab his elbow. Without looking, he spun around and with his other hand nailed Kalini in the face. She fell back and, as fate would have it, cut the back of her shoulder deeply on a sharp pointed tree branch behind her.

Amid the flurry of activity, no one had noticed her arrival.

T.J. could not believe what he had just done. Chandra immediately broke free and went to his sister. T.J., feeling terrible and scared but knowing he would not be able to mend anything, stared for a second. He then motioned to the other boys, who were also in shock and all three took off running. His lip bloodied, Chandra went to help his sister, who now had a swollen eye and an open wound on her shoulder.

Dr. Smith had just finished with his last patient and was about to leave when Kalini and Chandra arrived. Kalini was crying as she went to him. The lover in him embraced her to his chest. The doctor in him began to examine her face and wound. Her eyebrow had a split in it and was so swollen that she could only open her eye about twenty percent of the way, but it looked like there would be no long-term damage. Through a flood of tears, she explained what happened.

He then needed to examine her shoulder as well as her back and chest, thus requiring him to cut her shirt. His first view of her beautiful skin was a sorrowful one. The sharp branch had penetrated deeply, but she appeared to have full range of motion and no pain in the front. He could clean it up and she would be fine.

He listened while he dressed her wounds. Kalini was whimpering. Dr. Smith cried with her, though he was filled with indignation and wanted to "make those boys pay." Nevertheless, Kalini tried to defend them, saying they didn't know what they were doing when T.J. had hit her.

Chandra did not share his sister's sentiment. He was in another room fuming over that stupid American who'd attacked his sister. He was going to find that kid and repay every wound Kalini had: black eye, gash in the back, everything. For everything that happened to Kalini, he would make certain T.J. would get the same.

The next morning, Dr. Smith went straight to the police and the school, but he was too late. T.J. was already gone, and no one knew who the other boys were. After speaking with the police and an attorney, it was determined that prosecution at this point would be futile. Thus, T.J. and a couple of thugs got away with their crime. And, as with many crimes, they had intended to do it, but in the grand scheme of things and in the life of Chandra and Kalini, it could have been a small thing that would have eventually faded with memory. Little did they or any-one else know that T.J.'s little gang had also gotten away with the worst possible crime as well.

# CHAPTER 8

# TRAGEDY

---

## June–August 2016 India

D r. Smith and Kalini decided that they had waited long enough, and the very next week they were married.

There was no dowry, no festival, and not even one relative besides Chandra in attendance, but it was nonetheless a joyful occasion. All of Kalini's dreams were hoisted on the shoulders of Dr. Smith. He was a humble servant of the people, and the only person to whom he was more dedicated than his patients was Kalini herself. She loved him with all her heart and so looked forward to having a family together, regardless of their finances or position. Only death itself would be able to keep these two lovers apart.

One month to the day after their marriage, Chandra was working at the office when he saw Kalini with an extraordinarily large smile. Her eyes were large and glowing as Chandra had never seen them before. *What could be going on with her?* he wondered. As she ran to Dr. Smith, Kalini was holding a large box wrapped in green paper. The darker green bow revealed it was a gift. Seeing as there was no holiday or birthday, this caused no small amount of confusion among the men who observed her. Kalini's face, however, let them know that whatever the surprise was, it was going to be awesome.

While Kalini was bursting with excitement, Dr. Smith opened the box to find another, similar but smaller box inside. It too was wrapped in the same manner. Kalini, standing behind her love with her arms wrapped around him, was too excited to stay silent. She kept telling him, "Hurry up, hurry up."

Chandra knew he wasn't really part of the scene that was playing out before him, but since Kalini made no effort to remove him, he kept watching. He still couldn't comprehend the excitement exuding from his sister. *Why is she so happy?*

He heard Dr. Smith say playfully, "I'm trying to, but somebody gave me so many layers." Then he landed a kiss on her mocha lips.

He tore through layer after layer of boxes—four, to be exact—and came to the last unwrapped box, small, like one that would hold a fancy pen. Kalini was squeezing him with all her might, exploding on the inside with excitement. It was all she could do not to scream. Surprisingly, Dr. Smith still hadn't figured out what she was so happy about.

However, all his curiosity immediately changed to joy as he saw the ergonomically designed white plastic tube with two pink lines on it. Kalini was pregnant. Immediately they both let out triumphal yells, and Dr. Smith turned around and hugged his love, which was reciprocated. She surprisingly still had some residual pain from the deep cut that she'd sustained trying to defend her brother. But apart from that minor discomfort, the couple could not have been happier.

Chandra did not see the lines, but he was familiar enough with the ways of the world to know what had happened. He had to admit, the scene was cute: his sister's excitement, the gift wrapping, Dr. Smith's excitement. *My sister is pregnant.* Was he excited? Was he happy for her? Was he angry? After his encounter with T.J., Chandra had given up on any sympathy for Americans. All the thoughts of there being some good ones out there were gone. He hated all Americans and never wanted to see another. But he knew that was not possible. He loved his sister too much to never see her. And of course, he would need to see his niece or nephew. If there was one good American in the world, it had to be Dr. Smith. In this one case only, he could make an exception. But if he turned out to be as rotten as Chandra feared deep down... he did not know what he would do.

As time went on, pregnancy started to take its toll on Kalini. About seven weeks in, she started having headaches that became unusually severe. She was still able to function but not nearly at her previous pace. Dr. Smith examined her, and as far as he could tell she was just slightly dehydrated, and her blood glucose level was low. He instructed her to double the amount of water she drank and eat one extra meal per day.

This helped... for about a day. Then the headaches got worse, and she started to feel some soreness around her neck. By this time Dr. Smith was more concerned, and he decided to take her to the city hospital after seeing his last few patients.

Kalini lay down in an adjacent room to wait for him to finish up. Upon saying goodbye to his last patient, only about a half hour had passed, but when he went to get her, she was unconscious and unresponsive. He rushed over to her and found she had a shallow pulse, and when he looked at her neck more closely, he saw a red line following a blood vessel going towards her heart.

Immediately he knew that he had not cleaned the wound on her shoulder well enough—bacteria had festered inside her to the point where infection had finally taken root and now was spreading. He rushed to find some antibiotics to inject, which he immediately did. This might have saved her life twenty hours earlier, but now it was too late. Within the ten minutes it took to get to the hospital, she and their unborn baby were dead.

He held her close to him desperately, but no amount of love or antibiotics was going to bring her back. Their hopes and dreams of the past six months were dashed to pieces on that hot August day. He'd gotten her to the hospital, but it didn't matter. He wept bitterly in the room for half an hour.

Kalini was gone—that was bad enough—but was he to blame? Sure, he hadn't hurt her, but if he had cleaned her wound better, wouldn't she be kissing him right now? He should have noticed that her symptoms were not simply part of a difficult first trimester and given her antibiotics. When her shoulder pain did not completely subside after a month, should he have taken her to the hospital then? Should he have just taken her to the hospital in the first place? Why was he practicing medicine if he could not even save the person closest and dearest to him?

These questions plagued him like a cancer. Eventually he stopped crying, although the pain in his temples throbbed excruciatingly with every laborious heartbeat. He didn't know what his future held, but it didn't involve Kalini and it wouldn't involve India.

He went straight to Dr. Subramaniam, a colleague in an adjacent town, and without going into details, told her that he would be leaving immediately and needed a place to refer his patients to. Dr. Subramaniam was already tight on time, but being a wonderfully understanding woman, she told him that she would make sure his patients were taken care of.

He then went to his office—the place that he used to look forward to going to every day, the place where he'd helped so many people overcome their ailments, the place where he and Kalini had been building their lives—and he put a sign on the door. It succinctly stated that any patient who needed care would have to visit Dr. Subramaniam's office as Dr. Smith's office had closed and would not be reopening. He did not even take the time to put the office up for sale. He assumed someone would eventually contact him to purchase the building, but whether that happened or someone just took possession of it, he didn't care.

It was too painful for him to stay in India. There were far too many reminders of Kalini throughout the streets, in the buildings, under the trees, all of which would only break his heart further with memories of the one he loved. But before he left, Dr. Smith did make one personal visit. He visited Chandra.

He had to say goodbye to Chandra—not because he was a good employee, and not even because Chandra was his brother-in-law, but because he felt that he owed it to Kalini.

As the love between Dr. Smith and Kalini had blossomed, she had told him all her feelings about Chandra, how he was so tender and had been a target of bullying, how she had sacrificed everything in her life so that he would be fed, how she loved him like a sister and like a mother. During some of the two lovers' most intimate conversations, when they had opened their souls to each other as deep as they could be opened, Kalini often spoke of her little brother. For that reason alone, Dr. Smith knew that he could not leave without saying goodbye and without explaining what had happened. He also knew that it would not come without much pain and tears for both of them.

Navnit, half-awake and smelling of alcohol, answered Dr. Smith's knock on the door of the shanty. Dr. Smith's emotions immediately began to well up in him, and he fought back tears remembering how Kalini had described her childhood. He had to ask three times for Chandra before it registered with Navnit. As Navnit went back to get Chandra, Dr. Smith still did not know exactly what he would say. How do you tell someone that their sister, provider, protector, and mother had died? He had no time to think it through because Chandra was there in a moment.

His face was too much like Kalini's. It didn't matter that he hadn't the words to speak: as soon as he saw Chandra, he started sobbing.

Before Dr. Smith could get out a word, Chandra knew something was very wrong and had already assumed the worst. Why else would he have come without his sister, who had been by his side from the day the two were married? In fact, he could not ever remember a time when he had spoken with Dr. Smith without her.

Unpoetically, the words flew out of Dr. Smith's mouth, "She's gone." Those two words were all he could manage to get out between the sobs and gasps of air.

Chandra understood but asked anyway, "Where?"

There were a few moans of sorrow before the response came. The doctor looked up at Chandra and replied, "She's dead."

Chandra's mind went blank. This couldn't be. She was young, she was healthy. What could have happened? Immediately his thoughts went back to his parents, who long ago had been killed in an accident. It must have been some American who recklessly murdered her or ran her over on the side of the road. Or was it someone closer to her?

"That boy that hurt her..." said Dr. Smith with much difficulty.

"T.J.? He is back? Did he kill her?" said Chandra, with both indignation and surprise. It would have been very odd if T.J. had come back to town, though if he had, Chandra would undoubtedly kill him.

"No, no," Dr. Smith managed to say. "That cut on her shoulder, it wasn't cleaned well enough, and it killed her. I didn't see it coming. I was too late to save her. It was an infection."

*It was you!* thought Chandra, but he was too stunned in the moment to react violently. "But you're a doctor," Chandra said.

"And I won't be practicing here anymore. I am leaving today." Though tearful, Dr. Smith said this with enough resolve that Chandra understood this was the last time he would ever see him. Before he turned to leave, he added, "Here are the keys to the office. You are welcome to stay there if you like." And that was the last thing that young Chandra Sandeep ever heard Dr. Smith say.

Not that it mattered to Chandra—he wasn't going to miss him, except that he would miss the opportunity to burn his clinic with him in it. He stuck the keys in his pocket and went back to his room. His uncle, who didn't even know that Dr. Smith and Kalini had married, poked his head in to ask what all the racket at the door was. Chandra told him that it was some teacher from the school who was headed back to Australia and wanted to say goodbye. Navnit then went back to his room to continue drinking and lazing around.

*I knew it.* The words kept circling through Chandra's mind. *I knew it was Americans. They killed my parents, and now they've killed Kalini.* It wasn't just some unknown assailant; it wasn't even just T.J. What had Dr. Smith done to save her? *Nothing,* thought Chandra. *He said he loved my sister and wanted to help people. He took advantage of my sister for a few months for his own pleasure and got rid of her at the first opportunity. He's a doctor. He could have saved her. He would have saved her if he had cared. And T.J., he probably knew all along that he was going to kill my sister. I was just a piece of the plan. They're all murderers.* These were the thoughts running through Chandra's fragile mind. He ruminated over never talking to another American again... and revenge. He was getting angrier by the second when all of a sudden he started to cry.

Dr. Smith's first words came back: *She's gone.* He was never going to see his sister again. Amid his rage, he had not even contemplated why he was angry. He now had no family, and the person he loved, the only person who loved him, was gone and was never going to be a part of his life again.

After a few minutes, he grabbed his drawings and headed for Dr. Smith's office. There was a deadness to everything. The air felt dead. The trees felt dead. The dirt road, the cloudy sky, the singing birds, everything seemed dead. The clinic didn't seem much different.

He saw the sign posted on the door, and anger and pain filled the dead space inside him. It was a good trade, for it is better to feel pain and anger than to feel nothing at all.

He entered and looked around. This was it. This was the place where he would live for a time and make his art, the only place he had to turn to now. For, much like Dr. Smith, Chandra could not stay in the place where there were so many reminders of Kalini.

Over the course of his short life, Chandra had lost the people he could talk to, the people who would listen if he had a problem. Now there was no one, and finding someone else was off the table. So, from that moment on, it was only the canvas and the paper. He would speak to his art and never reveal his heart to another person, no matter how hard they may try.

He pulled a sketchpad from his portfolio and started a new drawing, but he didn't get far. As the pencil moved over the page, sorrow filled his heart. *Amma, Appa, and now Kalini. They are all gone!* A tear fell on the paper, and he tried to wipe it with his shaking hand. Graphite smeared on the page and his skin. He ripped the paper from the pad and tore it to pieces, and as he crumpled the pieces up, his emotions overcame him and he began to wail. He was alone, torn, stressed, and heartbroken.

He looked at the instruments on the counter. How easy it would be to use one of them to end his miserable life. Then he could be with Kalini. Then he would never need to worry about any Americans ruining his already ruined life.

He picked up a scalpel, examining its blade and the depth of the arteries in his wrists. It would be so easy. The knife quivered in his hand as he continued to contemplate his own end. Then he threw it against the wall.

His heart was pounding as he looked around the office. He went back to the counter and looked at all the supplies that were neatly laid out, things that his sister had put there. He put one hand on a jar of tongue depressors and another on a box of gloves and thrust them down the length of the counter. A cacophony of shattering glass ripped the air of the otherwise silent examination room. Then he was overcome with grief again, fell to his knees, and cried for hours. His poor mind was tormented by the demons of evil deeds done against his family and himself. He curled up on the floor and held his portfolio against his chest as he cried.

Then he heard Kalini's voice. He jumped to his feet. She was standing in the next room with the door open. Chandra couldn't believe his eyes. She wasn't gone after all! It had all been a dream. Elated, he went to her. She smiled, then put on a serious face. "Promise me, right now, that you will not start another fight with an American."

The elation was fleeting. Chandra stopped. It hadn't been a dream. Rage filled his heart like he never had felt before. He looked at Kalini. In life he never spoke to Kalini this way, but in death he did not need to worry about hurting her feelings or keeping her safe. It was too late for that. When he spoke, his emotions were as spirited as his words, "You're dead."

Kalini's face showed disappointment, "You promised me."

Chandra didn't care. His promises had done nothing. If he had broken his promise and protected her against those whom he knew were their enemies, she would still be alive. But she wasn't. Now it was time for a change. "You're dead. My promises to you are dead."

Kalini started to beg, "Please, Chandra."

This show of emotion had no effect on his resolve. Chandra slowly backed up as he watched his sister cry. "You're dead… Amma and Appa are dead… All of you were killed by Americans. I have no promises." His heart was pounding so hard as he defied his sister that he woke up, still lying on the floor with his portfolio clenched to his chest.

His hands were shaking so badly that he could not even wipe his tear-stained eyes. His mind was a whirlwind of pain. He was hurt, and he was going to make sure others hurt as well. Someone had to pay. Her death, along with the deaths of his parents, could not go unpunished, and if no one else was going to serve justice, he would. Previously he had decided that he would never speak to another American. That was going to change. Yes, he would inflict pain just the way he had seen Dr. Smith and T.J. do it. He would play the part of the innocent nice person, and just when they trusted him, he would strike. Now he just had to figure out when and how.

# CHAPTER 9

# STRANDED

---

## 2018–2019 India/Vietnam

Nearly two years had passed, and other than stupid, simple generic ideas, Chandra still did not have a plan for how he could exact his revenge. Notwithstanding his inability to formulate one, he was brilliant and decided he could learn more about infrastructure and weak points in society if he were to go to school. Thus, with his good grades and the surprising sale of a doctor's office, Chandra Sandeep was able to go to the prestigious Indian Institute of Technology.

When he arrived at the university, he dove in headfirst and flourished so that after two quick semesters he was ready to declare his major: materials science and mechanical engineering. Early in his sophomore year, he led a team of students in constructing a high-efficiency supercar for a competition funded by the American company Fuel and Renewable Technologies. The car was powered by a single-piston, single-stroke engine, similar to those found in common string weed trimmers. It rolled on three well-lubed wheels from an old wheelchair: two in the front and one in the back. His biggest problem was aerodynamics. He did not have anyone to mold him a low-drag fuselage, and he didn't have the money to pay for one even if he could find someone to make it. As a result, air resistance kept his fuel efficiency under 130 kpl (306 mpg), far below that of the currently produced super-efficient cars, which can approach 1,700 kpl. Notwithstanding his limited resources, it was a roaring success.

Impressed with precocious young Chandra, his materials science professor informed him of a lead on a coal mining internship in Vietnam. It was very enticing considering the group, which was university-affiliated, and which had also secured some land on which they hoped to drill for oil. The Vietnamese government showed much interest in the team's efforts and gladly offered them the land to do their research on, with the understanding that all the research would remain the intellectual and physical property of the Socialist Republic of Vietnam. In turn, they would grant the Indian Institute of Technology rights to do research over the next fifteen years.

This piqued Chandra's interest. Coal was good, but oil was even better. He knew that if Americans liked anything, it was driving cars and burning gas. This could be an in for him to get with an American company. Then he could figure out a way to do the rest. Chandra jumped at the idea and secured the necessary travel documents.

About one month before Chandra was to embark on his study abroad, the team finished their first drilling and retrieved some very light crude oil. A couple of days later, after testing the oil, they presented their first findings to the Vietnamese government, who drooled at the results and asked the researchers to determine the expected volume of the reserve.

Over the next three weeks, the team came to the conclusion, with about 75% confidence, that the reserve was indeed quite large—large enough to maintain a strong export supply for over twenty-five years, even taking into account increased worldwide consumption. With the report in hand, the government contacted several foreign investors. A company by the name of Petroleum and Oil Output Processing USA was granted access, under strict government supervision, to drill.

Though good for the pockets of the American company and the Vietnamese government, this abrupt sequence of events turned out to be very bad for the researchers and it proved far worse for Chandra. The company did not want college students mucking up the project, and the researchers no longer had a role to play. The Vietnamese government reneged on its deal to let the researchers continue their work and, furthermore, told them they had twenty-four hours to leave.

All this transpired while Chandra was already en route. By the time he arrived at the research site, one would not have even known that the Indian Institute of Technology had ever been there. A chain link fence surrounded the site, and a large sign read "USA", neither of which augured well for Chandra. Furthermore, he noticed that the large open field did not have a modest research drill but rather several bulldozers and cranes on site, as if commercial-scale work was about to start.

When Chandra tried to enter the former research site, he was told to get lost. After he explained the situation, a manager came to break the news to him. He was sickened when he heard an American company had destroyed his plans, but ruined plans were the least of his problems. Chandra had expected that when the project concluded, he would secure passage back to India with the rest of the research team. However, the team had already left, and no one had thought to make return travel arrangements for Chandra. He was now stranded in Vietnam with no money and no way home.

# CHAPTER 10

# Deep-Sea Fishing with Chandra

**2019 Vietnam/South China Sea**

Having lived with a constantly drunk uncle, Chandra had no interest in booze. But his dismally unfortunate and bleak situation, along with his having no particular place to go, prompted him to head into a bar. The exterior of the building was not much to look at: a shabby storefront that bore a few simple words in a partially Romanized language that he couldn't read and a sun-bleached and weather-worn painting of a martini. The interior was even less comely. The floor was dirt, and none of the bar stools matched. Small round tables dotted the dusty floor of what appeared to be an old stable. There were a couple of men who looked to be in their fifties at tables with women who looked to be in their twenties. Each of the ladies was wearing once red, now dirty brown high-heeled shoes and enough lipstick that even though Chandra could not understand the language, the incessant peeling apart of the lips let him know exactly what was being said. Each woman was caressing the hands and arms of the client she'd just met, doing her best to elicit a smile from herself and from her patron, for neither was happy. A few more women closer to forty years of age were waiting at the bar for some customers of their own.

The bartender's shirtless, overhanging gut concealed a knot in the hemp rope that held up his cheap scrub-type pants. His hands bore the scars of years of hard labor by means of which he had provided for his wife and six children. His scruffy face displayed the fatigue that came from working all day in fields, then late into the night at the bar. Lastly, but most poignant to Chandra, the mangled right side of his body bore witness to an atrocity of a war long past. It seemed inescapable: everywhere he went, Chandra was reminded that America leads to pain and suffering for others.

Chandra didn't need to speak Vietnamese to order a beer. The worn-out bartender had seen sad faces like his a thousand times before. He sat there crying, with a woman twice his age trying to rub his back. The bartender shooed her off and gave him one on the house.

About halfway through Chandra's Bia Hơi, a gentleman with clothing more appropriate for Wall Street than this bar came in smoking a Cuban cigar. Though the bartender did not recognize the man, he had seen enough sharks to immediately sense that this was bad news. The bartender spoke no Tamil, so he flicked his eyes toward the man and spoke the only English words he thought the young Indian at his bar might recognize: "No good."

The well-dressed man came close, sat down beside Chandra, and made an attempt to speak to him in Vietnamese without success. Like the bartender, he was unfamiliar with any Indian languages, so he tried his luck with English, in which he was semi-proficient.

He asked Chandra what was wrong, then listened attentively. He could not make out the details, but he understood enough to know that the young man was trapped without any money. He told Chandra he was a businessman and that he could help him find work down by the water to get some money to go back to India. Considering his indigent and hopeless situation, Chandra inquired further.

"You just helping the boats. The fishing boats," said the man in the suit.

"You want me to work on the docks?" asked Chandra.

"Yes, at docks. Easy money."

"How long will it take for me to get enough money?"

"Lot a money at the docks. You working hard. You have lot a money."

Chandra didn't trust that there would be a lot of money and knew well enough that the work would be difficult. But even if it was not that lucrative, he figured it was better than starving to death. So he and the gentleman started to leave, along with one of the younger hookers who left her prospect at the table for the wealthier-appearing "gentleman."

Before they reached door, the bartender barricaded the way of the party and got into an argument with the well-dressed man. He huffed out a couple of times in English, "No, bad." Chandra figured the man who was leading the way was probably not going to make any 100 Best Employers list, but he had no choice and was committed to go with him. It was then that the gentleman pulled out a pistol and yelled at the bartender to get out of the way, which he did. Chandra wanted to run but feared doing so would endanger his life as well, so he just stood there, petrified. The gentleman turned around, smiled, and showed Chandra and the young lady to the car, which had another man well-dressed man in the front seat.

The ride seemed a lot longer than it really was. In any other situation, Chandra could have enjoyed the beautiful scenery. But the lush forests of the Kon Ka Kinh National Park offered him little comfort on the journey down to Dong Da. The trembling hands and tears rolling down the cheeks of the young lady beside him confirmed that she, too, was scared.

Not five years older than Chandra, she had gotten involved with the wrong group of men once before, which led her down a career path that had destroyed her young life. She remembered her family: she'd grown up poor but always happy. She remembered the first time she sold herself, the pain and shame she had felt, and yet how others, her "new friends," had congratulated her for making her way in the world. Yet notwithstanding the horrible choices she had made in the past and the terrible and often gruesome experiences she'd had subsequently, she now feared things could be worse, much worse than ever before. Her quivering lips and her despondent looks out the window told Chandra that she wanted to be back home, to have a mom, to feel a hug and a kiss and hear an "Everything'll be all right"— the same things Chandra wanted. But both of them knew that wasn't going to happen. So, trembling and forlorn, she looked out her window, and frustrated and lonesome, he looked out his.

About three miles from the harbor, the gentleman, who still wore a smile on his face, led Chandra one direction while his accomplice led the young prostitute in another. He was taken to a room to spend the night. It was simple and not terribly clean. When Chandra went inside to look around, the door shut behind him and he heard it lock. He ran back to try the knob, but he knew before he got there that it wasn't going to open. Yelling was futile. Now, he was not only trapped in a country where he did not know the language, he was a prisoner. And soon enough, he would find out why. Though he could not figure out how, he had a strong inner feeling that an outside influence was to blame for his situation, and his constant nagging thought was that it had to be Americans. He walked over to a cot attached to the wall, lay on it, stared at the ceiling, shook his head, and sobbed.

After about an hour he fell asleep, only to be awakened two hours later by the sound of a gunshot. Silence followed the noise and he fell asleep again, but was awoken about thirty minutes later by the man who had led him from the bar. This time, he did not wear his usual smile, nor did his accomplice. Instead, he carried his revolver, which he pointed at Chandra, and, without any show of emotion, he said, "Move."

As Chandra was escorted back to the same car that had brought him there, he looked left and saw the pair of red high heels the young woman who'd left the bar with him had worn. They were sticking out from behind a dumpster, and her feet were still in them. Had it not been for the rage that was escalating moment by moment to get back at their mutual enemies, he would have bolted so as to get shot and thus join her and his sister in that other unknown land. But he had to live. Living was the only way that he could make sure that someone would pay. If he died, no one would remember or even care about any of them.

Chandra and his escorts arrived at the harbor, and he was taken to a raggedy fishing boat, where his headhunter said, "Here your new job," then laughed. The man watched, gun in hand, to make sure that neither Chandra nor any of the three other men in the same situation would try to jump.

The boat was captained by a man who referred to himself as "Skipper." Skipper had three other men who willingly worked for him. Then there were the other three men, all Vietnamese, whom Chandra could tell had been forced onto the boat, by either the same or another shark, to be slaves.

Chandra soon found that one of the willing workers spoke English. When he inquired what was going on, his new boss only grinned and said what Chandra already knew: they were going fishing; and that, they did.

For the next month, Chandra never saw land. They received fuel and provisions via other vessels, which, in turn, took their catch from a bloody cesspool on the lower deck that was full of dead fish, trimethylamine, plenty of sweat, and occasionally, vomit.

Day in and day out, for anywhere from sixteen to twenty-one hours a day, they caught fish. If the fishing was really good, they did not sleep at all. If the fishing was bad, they got some sleep, but only after the frustrations of Skipper were appeased by furiously yelling and slapping the slaves. The bulk of the food brought on board was consumed by Skipper and his mates. The four slaves received small portions twice a day.

After the first week, one of the slaves started yelling. Chandra did not know exactly what he was saying, but he was certain he felt the same way. The man, who looked to be in his early thirties, was exhausted and hungry. Chandra watched as the crew motioned him to get back to work. Out of his wits and out of strength, he vehemently refused, at which point the crew member gritted his teeth, grabbed him by the throat, and threw him to the deck. He still showed signs of reluctance, and the same crew member grabbed him by the scruff of the neck and took him into the cabin, followed by the other two taskmasters.

Chandra's heart was wrenched at every scream for the next fifteen minutes as his slave-mate was beaten and tortured. When he came back to the upper deck of the boat, he had bruises across his chest, cuts all over his back, and wounds around his eyes and mouth. His newly acquired awkward gait let everyone else know that even his most secret parts had not been spared by these savages.

About a week after this event, all four captives were extremely weary from the tremendous volume of albacore tuna they had been catching. They had started the day at around 3:45 a.m. and it had been more or less nonstop. It was now 9:45 p.m. and the fishing hadn't let up.

The same man who had been tortured and beaten seven days prior collapsed. He couldn't work any longer. A crew member yelled for him to get to his feet. He was conscious, he was alive, but he wasn't able to get up. He was kicked a few times, and he moaned with each kick, but that was all he could do. He couldn't fight back; he couldn't talk back. His strength was depleted and his mind was no longer coherent. He could only lie there and take it.

The same crew member went and got the Skipper. He examined the man, and as his henchman had told him, found him completely useless. He pulled out a knife and poked holes in the man's larynx, and the two of them threw him overboard. Even the best swimmers, who can hold their breath for minutes, would have been able to do little to keep water out with holes in his throat, so this man, bereft of breath and spirit, had no chance. But it didn't matter. Even without holes in his throat, he would have gladly inhaled the cool, lethal salt water to end his life.

Chandra finally asked, "Why do you need all this fish?"

The crew member who could speak English grinned the same grin he had when Chandra first got on the boat and said, "Americans like tuna."

*I knew it*, Chandra thought. All the death that he had seen was the result of American gluttony. How he wished he could be free, gun in hand, to walk the streets of New York—or even better, to be in a restaurant with tuna in one hand and a gun in the other, serving poetic justice along with all the food they wanted. Then he would let Americans know how he felt. Then he would avenge all the wrongs he'd suffered and witnessed: his dad, his mom, Kalini, her unborn child, the young lady, and his co-worker. Then he would be at peace. But alas, he was on a fishing boat, helping satisfy Americans' appetites and bolstering an economy of human trafficking. If he lived to see land again, this would make for a very interesting drawing.

"Some of the tuna are already spoiled," Chandra said to the crewman.

"Maybe take it out later, maybe not. You put it in a can, Americans never notice. They eat anything; they don't know where it come from."

Chandra fished almost incessantly for the next week and a half. In one small respect, he felt fortunate: Fish was the one type of animal flesh that he had consumed growing up. Whenever he managed to keep a fish from making its way down to the reddened water of the lower deck, he would use his bare hands to remove the skin and eat the flesh while the crew slept. The problem was the crew did not sleep every night. Even so, the fish sustained him. He was smart enough to let the other indentured servants sleep so that no one knew he was eating, and during the day, he did not let his added strength show, he just kept pace with the others. It was still difficult, but his age and his desire for vengeance pushed him to go on.

By the end of that week, it was 39°C (103°F) a very strange temperature on the water, and it had been nearly that hot for three days. None of the men on board was working as hard as normal, and neither Skipper nor his minions were enforcing the rules today. They didn't have adequate drinking water, and one of the slaves had already vomited. Chandra was more tired than he had ever been in his life. The boat needed supplies, or everyone was going to join their friend who had been thrown overboard two weeks earlier. At dusk, everyone went to sleep.

Hunger and thirst had taken control of the ship, and Skipper navigated to get closer to the shore than he ever had. It was a risk he had to take, or provisions may not get to them in time. After about two hours of sleep, Chandra awoke, found a small fish, and started to devour it just north of its lateral line. He realized just how worn out, delusional, and close to death he was when he saw something sparkling on the water. The nights he'd spent over the last month had gotten him accustomed to seeing starlight on a glassy sea, but this was different. There was a small chop that wouldn't allow for any reflection of stars, notwithstanding the clearness of the night sky.

He kept eating. He rubbed his eyes. Either he was dead already, or there were lights, and they were close. They could not have been more than two or three miles away. If he did not act now, he knew he would be dead within a month's time.

He stole away to where the fresh water was kept. There were only about three hundred milliliters left. He grabbed it and drank it down. On the way out, he stumbled and looked up in horror. A crew member was staring him right in the eye from his bunk. He would have to make a run for it out of the cabin.

He got to the door but did not hear any hustling or other footsteps. When he looked back, he saw no one following him. With great relief, he realized the man was dead. Chandra grinned the same grin that he had received from the dead man previously, then used the time to eat a double portion of meat. When he finished and had as much strength as he thought he could realistically expect, he dove into the water.

Chandra had always been a good swimmer, and working like a dog for the last month had made him strong, but his glycogen stores were at a minimum and his hydration levels were too low to swim hard. Even though it would take about three times longer, he decided to backstroke.

It was a long night for Chandra. Every bit of chop on the dark sea looked like a shark fin coming at him. Even in this heat wave, the water felt like ice, and he had no energy to warm himself. Even using this lazy stroke, his arms were burning after thirty minutes.

After an hour, Chandra decided to float and make sure he was still headed towards his mark. His heart sank when he saw the lights. They still seemed an eternity away. Vengeful or not, he wasn't going to make it. He was worn out. He felt like he could go a little further physically, but mentally he had had enough; it was time to quit. He stopped his slow cadence of strokes, and his feet started to sink. Soon, the cool, refreshing water would wipe away the fatigue and heartbreak. His parents, his sister, the young prostitute, and his fellow slave were all about to welcome their friend, and he was glad of it.

All of a sudden, he was startled by the call of a horn. It was just like the one that he had heard sound a few times on the boat that had stolen the last thirty days of his life. In fact, it was the same. If he was going to die, he certainly was not going to allow himself to die at the hands of those pirates. His heart took courage, and his arms began paddling again. Two miles and two and a half hours from the spot where he'd started, a wave broke and threw Chandra onto a beach. He lay there, motionless.

He was unconscious, badly dehydrated, and all his skin was shriveled, but he wasn't dead. He was alive on Shangchuan Island.

# CHANDRA'S IDEA

**2019 China**

The first crimson rays of sunlight were illuminating the eastern sky over the Pacific Ocean when ten-year-old Dong Xi was playing with his dog, Le Hau, on the khaki sand adorning Shangchuan Island beach. He had to admit that it had been a pretty good vacation so far, even if they had not gone to Tokyo Disneyland like he wanted. There is an ethereal connection between nature and little boys, one that Dong Xi's parents wanted to cultivate as a counter to the sea of video games that their son was growing up in.

There was a five-mph wind out of the northeast that caught Le Hau's attention, and instinctively he took off running. Dong Xi called for his doggie to come back, to no avail. Then, far north of Dong Xi, he could see what his dog had already smelled: some sort of animal had beached itself during the night. *Could it be a giant turtle?* thought little Dong Xi. For a young man of his age, a discovery of this immensity couldn't wait, and straight away, both he and his dog were running towards this amazing adventure.

About a hundred yards short of his destination, Dong Xi noticed that it was no animal at all but a person. His stride slowed down due to innate apprehension, but being a generally sweet and helpful boy, he kept going because he knew this person either was dead or needed help.

As he neared, he thought the young man appeared dead. Seeing a dead person would be scary, but still would be an adventure, so he kept approaching. But then he saw movement from this driftwood body when it was licked on the face by Le Hau. Dong Xi knew that the stranger still had life in him but perhaps would not for long without assistance. Dong Xi stopped where he was, then ran back to get his father.

When they both returned, for the first time in five weeks, Chandra was in good hands. Dong Xi's family currently lived in Hong Kong, and Dong Xi, being the son in a very wealthy family, had the best education one could hope for. His father owned several manufacturing facilities, and being intimately aware of how much of his products were made for export, he was determined that Dong Xi should become fluent, or at least proficient, in English. To this end, there was always an American or British nanny in the house. Thus, Dong Xi could easily communicate with Chandra.

Even though Dong Xi was just a boy without a snippet of malign intent, Chandra had become completely jaded towards strangers, and he did not want to give more information away than was absolutely necessary. He said only that he needed food and a way back to India.

Food was easy. Dong Xi's father brought him to the beach house they were renting for the week and fed him the same expensive cuisine that he had purchased for his own family. Dong Xi's father, who in fact spoke English quite well himself but lacked confidence for casual conversation, had his son ask Chandra whether they could give him some clothes. It was then that Chandra noticed just how bad he looked. The rags that had once been his shorts were so frayed and filthy that the casual onlooker would have been hard pressed to guess what the original length and color had been. The t-shirt that he had been given on the boat was so stained with fish slime and blood that it cracked now that it was dry. He took them up on the offer of clothes, and he took a bath as well, but it would be several more baths before the fish oil was removed from his pores, and commensurately, the smell as well.

As for a way back to India, that was harder, a lot harder. Having been a slave for the past month on a boat in the South China Sea, as far as any government was concerned, Chandra didn't exist: no visa, no passport, no ID. The only option he had to was to contact the university and his professors, who had assumed he was either trapped in Vietnam or dead, to get some paperwork sent to him. This wasn't going to happen overnight; in fact, it wouldn't happen that month.

Luckily, he was safe with Dong Xi's family. With his assortment of business ties, Dong Xi's father secured work for Chandra. About twenty kilometers west of their home in the outskirts of Hong Kong was a factory that turned a unique raw material into a highly specialized product. It was a clean, state-of-the art facility, and Dong Xi's father was the owner, as much as one can be in China, so even if others in the factory didn't think they needed another employee, they had to take Chandra anyway.

On his first day on the job, Chandra was suited up with a white smock, a thin white hair net, and nitrile gloves. He was then stationed next to a conveyor to inspect millions of duck feathers as they passed by. His job was to remove large pieces of foreign material before the feathers went for further cleaning and extraction. Chandra was a brilliant young man, but he could not for the life of him figure out why on earth anyone would need so many duck feathers. It could not have been for any cushioning or woven material, for the feathers went through some sort of extraction process. They were getting some chemical constituent out of it, but what?

While he stood there watching the countless feathers go by, he saw a clump of tangled hair. He dutifully grabbed it and threw it into the rubbish bin beside him that was marked for waste. To his surprise, he saw another clump of hair about a minute later. This he also removed, and he continued to do so for the next five minutes until a supervisor came by.

Upset but unable to communicate, the foreman grabbed the rubbish bin and dumped the hair back on to the line. So, from that moment on, Chandra removed only rocks and feces and left the hair on the line. All the hair was black, and some of it was curly, indicating it came from all parts of the body. It was definitely human, not animal. He let it pass and was left to wonder what the end product was.

A few days later, he saw the finished goods with English writing on the kraft paper bags. It read, "L-cysteine monohydrate FCC USP." Now he knew what it was, an amino acid, but he couldn't decipher the rest of it. He did, however, assume that USP had something to do with America. At this point, seeing that Americans would stoop so low as to use human hair didn't surprise him. His assumptions were confirmed when an American auditor named Dave Jackson came to the facility.

Dave Jackson spent most of his time in an office sorting through paperwork, but he did observe the production floor for about two hours. He briefly passed by Chandra, and thinking he was speaking to himself, he said, "He must be a long way from home."

Seeing an American in China sent chills through Chandra's body. How many of the lives of those he knew or loved had suffered for him and his ilk? How terrible his life had been because of them! He could lash out at the man and sink his teeth into the man's face or throat. Or better yet, he could knock him unconscious and send his hair down the conveyor, still attached to his body, to be burned in the heated broth to make cysteine. Chandra had had thoughts of pain and even death previously, but these thoughts, so instinctive now, were of a baser sort. They came so quickly. He loathed Americans. They were his enemy. All the crying he'd done, all the bullying he had experienced, all the death that he had witnessed... It was Americans. His subconscious had recognized this fact first. Now his mind was no longer surprised by his bloodlust. It was a part of him.

The problem was that Dave Jackson was about seventy pounds heavier than Chandra and not much fatter. Chandra knew he wouldn't have a chance in a physical altercation with this man. So he faked a pleasant face—the kind Kalini had always worn because she was good, the one the Chandra would need to do the most harm. He smiled and inquisitively asked, "What do you want with all this cysteine?"

Dave was shocked and a little embarrassed that he had incorrectly assumed that no one would understand him. He was also very confused about why a young English-speaking Indian man was working in a Chinese factory. Dave looked back and matter-of-factly answered Chandra's question, "Dough and flavors."

Chandra was flabbergasted. "Bread dough?"

"You got it."

"You eat this?"

"Just in small amounts. It really improves the texture of the dough, and it's a key ingredient in creating some natural flavors."

Chandra's thoughts were a mix of amazement, confusion, hatred, and, surprisingly, some satisfaction. His mind was clouded with hatred, blaming Americans for all sorts of evils, but he still had acute clarity of mind for logic. It seemed incredible that Americans were so monstrous as to actually eat people.

"Do they know what it comes from?"

"We don't like to know all the details. We just want safe food at a low price."

Upon hearing the word *safe*, a smile inched its way over Chandra's face and diabolical seeds of mischief were planted in his mind. He remembered the words of the slave master on the ship, "Americans will eat anything." That man and the auditor were right. As long as they don't know the details, Americans will eat whatever is put in front of them. All of a sudden, Chandra knew what he needed to do.

That evening, he started a new drawing for his portfolio, not realizing he was also drawing plans for the rest of his life.

# CHAPTER 12

# TIME TO MOVE

**2019–2021 India/United States**

For the first time in a very long time, Chandra Sandeep had direction in his life. The series of misfortunes that had befallen him had given him a better understanding of a very strong and influential segment of the American economy. This segment was vulnerable due to its lack of transparency. It was also incredibly complex: even a purchase as simple as bread or candy required the use of ingredients from all over the world. It was a stark contrast to the markets where Kalini had bought their food—food that, for the most part, had come from within a one-hundred-kilometer radius.

Chandra knew that doing something to the food Americans eat would be extremely impactful. He also knew that anything he did could affect anyone—a child, a baby, the elderly. But it didn't matter. Looking back over his life, he couldn't believe that he hadn't seen it before. His parents had been killed while working on an American food plantation. Kalini was killed by the son of someone working for an American food company. Then, most recently, a young prostitute and a slave had both been killed in the service of providing Americans with food. And Chandra was just one person. The death toll in reality had to be immense.

He had seen firsthand how a strong economy could be nonchalant about the lives of others, and he knew that to make them pay, he would need to be nonchalant as well.

So, during his time in China, he learned as much as he could about the food industry by working with Dong Xi's father, transferring to other factories to see their operations as well. It was mostly ingredients used in small quantities for baking: ascorbic acid, enrichment nutrients, and the like. All the facilities were very clean and well supervised. He assumed that would be the case in the States as well. Thus, it became apparent that he would not be able to just waltz into any factory he chose and do whatever he wanted. If food, which had plagued him from his infancy, was to be the vehicle for his wrath, then he would have to work quietly from within, gaining trust and finding the weak spots. And if he wanted to increase the reach of his payback, he would need help.

Ten months later, the papers came with some money so that Chandra could make his way back to India. His first priority was to finish his degree and get to the States. But how? How could a young Indian man with no family emigrate to the US on his own? He would have a degree, but nothing else.

Chandra knew now what sort of weapon of mass destruction he would use. Now, he needed only to calculate the details of his plan. What food would be the best target? Where was security in the system the weakest? Where could he get help? How could he reach as many people as possible? To this end, he changed his major from materials science and engineering to food science and engineering.

Chandra's hatred and rage did not lessen his academic prowess, and he found it delightfully easy to do well in his new discipline. This did not cause him to be lackadaisical in his studies, however. He was a machine. He devoured his classes to find out all the intricacies of food processing, all the while looking for the best spots to put his diabolical plan into action. Unlike most students, he read every book assigned for his classes cover to cover, and at least one additional food engineering or manufacturing book each week. But it wasn't enough. It soon became apparent that all the books and classes were about how to manufacture food, how to preserve food, how to make food more nutritious, or how to make it safer—the opposite of his intention. He had learned more about the mechanics and weaknesses of the industry aboard a slave ship in the Indian Ocean and in a few ingredient factories in China than he had from all the books he'd read during his first month in school. He concluded that the only way to find the information he needed was to get inside the processing facilities.

This was not an easy task for a young man in India. Though the trend toward a more Western style of food consumption was still in its early stages, most Indians were still preparing food in their own homes. Therefore, large food processing plants were scarce. The area surrounding him was devoid of them except for a couple of grain mills, which he had already seen, and none of that grain would be headed to the US.

As graduation started knocking on his door, so did some of his professors, encouraging him to go to the US for a PhD. He was told that an American degree would guarantee him the kind of position he wanted anywhere in the world, especially if he wanted to teach. He didn't need much convincing. A good career meant nothing to him, but getting an inside glimpse of the US, learning the quality assurance standards maintained in the factories, observing production on their own turf, and pinpointing the weak points of the American industrial food infrastructure was a malevolent dream come true.

His grades, his command of English, and the charm he'd learned from Kalini made him a shoo-in at any land-grant food science program. The very healthy sum of money that the government of India sent with him didn't hurt, either. Even without expertise in American food production and consumption, he knew enough of the basics to guide his graduate program choices. First and foremost, everyone knew that the

United States is the world leader in the production of wheat and corn. The term *breadbasket*, while not well known in India, was known to his advisors. Thus, seeing America's breadbasket as a critical area to map out, he applied to the University of Nebraska.

In India, the US, and several other parts of the world, milk production is extremely high to meet growing populations' demands for protein and sweets. It is no surprise, then, that fluid milk is in the top five of agricultural products worldwide. Having ties to both fluid milk and cheese research, Chandra also applied to the University of Wisconsin.

Much of the fruit and vegetables sold in the US is imported, but of all the domestic production, California carries a disproportionate load. Domestic tomatoes and almonds, especially, call California home. With this in mind, and the potential to see an old friend, he applied to the University of California, Davis.

Lastly, he applied to both Cornell and Penn State universities due to their proximity to New York City.

All five schools readily accepted him, and at least one professor from each of their respective food science programs was more than happy to bring him in to join their team of researchers.

In the end, it was UC Davis.


When Chandra stepped onto the Boeing 777 that would eventually take him to America, he was well aware that he was touching Indian soil for the last time. He didn't know the details yet, but he knew that this would be a one-way ticket. One way or another, his life was going to end in America. But until that time, he would figure out how to get others, many others, to die first.

United Airlines allowed one checked bag and one carry-on, but all Chandra needed was the carry-on. Just a small suitcase with two pairs of pants, four shirts, some underwear, his art portfolio, and a mind full of malice was all that Chandra Sandeep brought with him to the United States.

When he stepped off the plane, just as he suspected, the air stank. He could not put his finger on the scent, but it was rotten like putrid flesh. In reality, there was no odor, and certainly the pollution here was no worse than the hazy sky and lack of sanitation he had been exposed to in Mumbai, whence he had departed. But he believed he was smelling something real, and it foreshadowed the carnage that he was to inflict. He breathed in deeply and exhaled with a malicious smile.

One of the first things he needed to do was locate the apartment he'd arranged to rent. He couldn't do what most other students in his situation did, that is, check out Craigslist for a roommate. He needed to be alone. He just needed a place to sleep, eat, and plan. Four walls and an internet connection would suffice, preferably away from other students.

He'd found such a place about seven miles from campus. When he saw it in person for the first time, he was very pleased. It was a fairly secluded old house with a studio apartment in the basement. Above lived an old woman who was perpetually absent visiting grandchildren or living in her Florida home. It was perfect.

A small kitchenette with a bar took up the first part of the west wall. It was followed by a very small bathroom that smelled of mildew due to lack of proper ventilation and cleaning. The north wall and most of the east wall were concrete with tiny windows at about neck height. However, in the middle of the east wall, there was a fireplace—or, rather, what used to be a fireplace, but the owners had sealed off the chimney and bricked up the opening to eliminate a fire hazard. The hearth, the woodwork, and the mantel were all intact, and though he'd had no such thing as a fireplace in the shanty he grew up in, something about it, perhaps the simplicity, reminded him of home. The mantel seemed a perfect spot for something special: his artwork.

Aside from the kitchenette and the bathroom, the floor was covered with dense industrial carpet. There was room for a bed, but he just used a pad that he rolled up during the day. The only furniture that would adorn the room was a small desk and a clothing drawer.

Soon after his first appraisal of his new home, it was time for dinner. Chandra put down his few things and made his way down the street towards the Quick and Easy Supermarket. He was shocked. Except for some vegetables in one corner, meat and fish in another, and a small bakery counter, everything was in a package. He took a glance at the checkout lanes. There were apples, potatoes, and a few canned goods, but by and large people were buying food in boxes.

He decided to get a firsthand look and strolled down an aisle full of these brightly colored boxes. Up to this point, he had assumed that every box was a full meal, and some were, but most were just part of a meal. There were cake mixes that came in boxes. There were graham crackers in boxes. And he saw boxes of something he had never heard of before, called stuffing. *What could it be stuffed with*, he wondered. He grabbed the box to take a closer look. There, on the box's narrow side, he saw the most wonderfully long recipe he had ever beheld in his life. It was the ingredients list, and actual food comprised very little of it. Vitamins, flavors, flavor enhancers, and preservatives comprised a healthy or perhaps unhealthy portion. Only a few ingredients could really be recognized as food. *As long as they don't know the details*, he thought. One corner of his mouth raised a little.

He still had no clue why such a thing was called stuffing, but he put it back anyway and decided to go to the exotic sea of packages that lay behind cold, clear glass. It was the biggest frozen food section he had ever encountered, and he could not believe that Americans were so lucky as to have this much electricity at their disposal. He also wondered why Americans used so many preservatives in things in the other aisle when they had all these wonderful freezers.

As he passed packages of imitation crab meat and fish sticks, notwithstanding his internal hatred, he soon couldn't help but feel giddy. It was as if he had walked onto the set of *Willy Wonka and the Chocolate Factory*, a film he had seen in an English class in high school. Ice cream came in all sorts of colors, all sorts of sizes, all sorts of shapes, and with all sorts of accessories. Some of it was pink and some of it was green. Some was in a tub and some was in a box. Some was on a stick and some was in a cone. Some was between two cookies and some was completely covered in chocolate. It was the most amazing assortment of desserts he could ever have imagined. He wanted to buy some, but after his experience in the other aisle, he decided to just get vanilla. Surely that would be simple.

He grabbed a carton of vanilla ice cream and marveled at how it had been made into such a shape. He assumed the ingredients would be cream, vanilla, sugar, and perhaps salt. He was right, but he also saw cornstarch, modified food starch, carboxymethyl cellulose, guar gum, locust bean gum, mono- and di-glycerides, polysorbate 80, and natural and artificial flavors.

*It's vanilla—how can it be so complicated?* he wondered. Then he chuckled at the word *artificial*, considering it humorous that you can actually tell people that a food is not real and they will still eat it. He put it back with the feeling that his work here in the US would be a lot easier than he had anticipated.

He found some dehydrated beans and rice in another aisle, then headed back to the produce so that he could get something he could actually eat. The apples he picked up were a lot shinier than what he was used to, but he didn't think much about it. He grabbed what he needed for the next few days and went to the checkout counter. He stood out like a sore thumb: a dark, thin island of pulses, fruits, and vegetables in a sea of semi-synthetic food being purchased by white, semi-overweight people. He smiled.

The cashier appreciated Chandra's cheery countenance and asked what made him so happy.

He responded, "This is my first time in an American grocery store. It is amazing!"

The sweet middle-aged woman said, "Well, come back and see us again."

He smiled again. "I'm sure I'll be back one way or another."

# PART II

# CHAPTER 13

# THE AMERICAN DREAM

## 1968 Southern California

When Carlos and Lucia Gutierrez emigrated from their longtime home of Michoacan, Mexico, they had more than the clothes on their backs, they had a pair of pants on their legs and socks on their feet, but that was it. Two failed businesses in their native land and the fantastic stories of successful immigrants in the land of opportunity lured them north to the United States.

Undeterred by their circumstances and with a stroke of luck, they both landed jobs cleaning at the Anaheim Convention Center. Lucia, unbeknownst to her, had just conceived, and eight months later they had three poor mouths to feed. Carlos, whose father had taught him the lessons of manhood from an age long since past, was too steeped in tradition to allow his wife to work with a newborn. But the loss of income was more than they felt they could afford if they wanted to live the American Dream. So, in the words later coined by George W. Bush and rehashed by Michael Moore, he did something "uniquely American" and took on a second job in the evening doing maintenance at the Sheraton next door.

Sleep-deprived though he was, Carlos succeeded phenomenally. Day in and day out, he worked tirelessly to support his family and build a nest egg. It wasn't easy, but they considered it a sacrifice worth making for a roof over their heads in a safe neighborhood. His hard work paid off in more ways than one. Within five years, he quit the Convention Center for a job as head of maintenance at the Sheraton. Suddenly, he had far more time on his hands and more money in his pocket than ever before. As such, he started to spend more time with his beautiful wife, who had stood by him faithfully, notwithstanding the fact that most of his time at home had been passed sleeping. He also enrolled in some business classes at Cal State Fullerton. After a bachelor's degree and ten more years, Carlos found himself the general manager of the Sheraton. But the business world was not the only place that Carlos and Lucia had found success: in those fifteen years, they had also produced five beautiful children: Tina, Carlos, Patricia, Maria, and Mateo.

Being the youngest, Mateo was the least pampered by mom and dad and received the most attention from his siblings. Although he was five years Carlos's junior, his older brother Mateo had taught him the fundamentals of wrestling, or at least what it feels like to be pounded. His two immediate older sisters often made him the object of their innate mothering instincts by playing house with him and, of course, he was always the baby. Diametrically opposed, these two training methods enriched the life of young Mateo. The fun of rough-and-tumble play he learned from his brother, and the need to care for one another he learned from his sisters. These lessons were anchors that he kept throughout his life and eventually led him to the perfect position to protect those around him.

In 2001, Mateo was on top of the world. Indeed, he was the epitome of the American dream. His parents' humble beginnings were a thing of the past, a thing quite foreign to his current comfortable life. In school, he was by no means a contender for valedictorian, but being ranked 69th out of a class of 377 was nothing to take lightly. But, as smart as he was, grades were not what Mateo was known for. Sports was where he excelled.

For the first eleven years of his life, he followed the same regimen that his brother and many other Latino immigrants followed: he played soccer.

He was signed up for his first soccer league three weeks before he turned four. By the time he was six, he was playing three seasons per year. He played the sport well, but he was not outstanding, except for one thing: his sprint. There may have been other kids on the field who could outrun him, but Mateo possessed the ability to go from a stand-still to full sprint in what seemed like less than half a step. His coaches noticed this unusual acceleration, and one of them told his father that he might be more suited for the basketball court than for the soccer field. The coach may have been right, but life took young Mateo away from the hardwood and placed him on the gridiron.

It was the second day of his fifth-grade year when this abrupt change took place. Kids on the playground were still sorting themselves into cliques that would last the entire school year. The wallflowers migrated to the red brick of the south side of the school to chit-chat the time away. The science-minded kids found that using sticks to dig holes near the fence uncovered all sorts of subterranean life forms to add to their collections of specimens. And the main body of children were engrossed in a seemingly endless game of co-ed tag—the game where the seeds of romance are sown, where young people can touch the arm of the one they love and shout, "You're it!"

Another group of nine boys were tossing around a football. It was an especially important year for them. Their hands were big enough now to use a large leather football at recess. Next year, they would be old enough for Pop Warner. They had one problem, though: everyone at that age wanted to throw the ball. Therefore, no one liked the idea of being quarterback. So when Bobby Kern, a soccer acquaintance of Mateo's, saw him reluctantly on the outskirts of the game of tag, he asked Mateo to play to even up the teams.

Mateo was not the least bit fond of the idea except that it would get him away from the wretched game of tag that he cared for even less. Football was a "gringo" sport, and suffice it to say, he had never so much as touched a football of that sort, let alone made any attempt to catch or throw one. But being intrepid also means a lot to an eleven-year-old boy, so he put on a face as confident as he could muster and joined Bobby's team.

The learning curve for Mateo as he figured out the basics of school-yard football was extremely steep. It had to be in order to avoid looking like an idiot and annoying his newly acquired friends. After one play, he learned that "hike" means you run forward, wave your hands, and say, "I'm open," and when the guy who throws the ball does not throw it to you, you chide him for overlooking someone who was "wide open." On the second play, he learned that before hike, no one can stand in front of the guy throwing the ball unless he uses a weapon, and he always chooses a shotgun. On his third down, he sprinted across the field and found that David, the boy who had chased him, was nowhere near him. Being "wide open," the most terrifying thing that could have happened, happened. The ball was thrown to him. The only times he had ever caught a ball were either in a baseball mitt or when he subbed in as goalie, neither of which he had done very often. As the ball came towards him, he reached up and touched it, but it went right through his hands and nailed him in the face. Everyone laughed, and Mateo felt like the biggest loser of the year or maybe even the century.

As the game pressed on, no more passes were thrown in Mateo's direction, and he did not feel any worse for it. In fact, he could not wait for his one day in humiliation boot camp to be over, and then they would never ask him to play again. The bell rang, heralding his freedom forever from the game of American football—but then Joey, their quarterback, said, "Last play! If we get a touchdown we win!" They were so far away from the end zone that there wasn't really any chance, and even though he didn't care at this point, Mateo did something that drastically changed his adolescent life.

Joey yelled out, "Hike," and Mateo took off straight down the field. He figured he could run farther away than Joey could throw, so it seemed a safe bet to save himself from a life of being ostracized. Just as before, no one was near him, partly because no one saw a need to cover him and partly because no one could have kept up with him anyway. For a split second, Joey talked himself out of throwing to Mateo, but it was just too tempting. No one else even had a chance at a touchdown, and Mateo was already almost twelve yards downfield. Joey went against his own good advice: he took the opportunity to show his arm strength, and he let it fly to Mateo.

Mateo's heart was pounding like it never had before. He had accepted enough passes in soccer to know not to break stride. This time, he even had to speed up a little, but an extra burst of energy to his legs was nothing new.

The spectators today, however, were new. It was embarrassing enough to have the eyes of the nine guys who'd asked him to play on him. But now that recess was over, everyone, even their teacher, Mrs. Newburg, was staring at him.

He kept his eyes on the ball. It seemed like the ball was racing him, so he threw all his energy into his legs, got underneath the ball, put his hands out, closed his eyes, and wrapped his arms around the first thing that touched them. But alas, he tripped, and the water-starved Southern California ground shrouded him in a cloud of dust when he tumbled to the ground.

As soon as the dust cleared, he saw nine boys shouting exuberantly about twenty yards back. For a moment he thought it must have been the laughter of seeing a dork trip and get hit by the ball, but there it, was in his arms. He had caught the pass. He didn't score a touchdown, they didn't win the game, but he had never felt so cool in all his days of playing soccer. Joey was the first to invite Mateo back to play again the next day, and by December he was the best receiver on the playground.

Mateo started lifting weights when he was thirteen and joined the freshman football team the next year. After the first two games, however, the coach would not let him stay, and he was put on junior varsity, where he was able to catch for over a thousand yards. At the end of the JV season, there were two games remaining on the varsity schedule, and the varsity coach asked Mateo whether he would like to play. He jumped at the offer and caught five passes.

The next three years brought Mateo success and accolades galore. As a sophomore, he caught just over 700 yards—708, to be exact—and scored seven touchdowns. In his junior year, he broke 1,000 yards and tallied 11 touchdowns. His senior year, the 2000 football season, was lights out with 1,544 receiving yards and 22 touchdowns. He was honored as Orange County Player of the Year and received offer letters to play at schools all over the US. But he chose to stay close to home, and he became a Trojan.

So, in 2001, Mateo was indeed on top of the world. He had just become part of a school he felt would return to greatness on the gridiron; he had a new, exciting, former NFL coach; and he seemed to have no apex to his skill level. During summer training, he managed to get his forty-yard dash down to an amazing 4.33. This was especially impressive considering that he had put on fifteen pounds of muscle since the last football season.

He was a coach's dream, but he was given a backup position to a few senior wideouts. Nevertheless, he was guaranteed thirty minutes of play, and the coach promised him he would be given a starting position if he excelled. It seemed that nothing could stop Mateo's blossoming as a player, and before long he would surely be in the NFL.

But right after his freshman season started, the tragedy of September 11 changed everything for young Mateo. It wrenched his soul that the country that had raised him and given his family the opportunity to escape poverty had been so mercilessly savaged by terrorists. As the weeks went by, he watched the developing scene of the war on terror unfold. The reports of US troops fighting in Afghanistan while he was on the practice field bothered him out of his wits. He could not go on with the semester. He gave up his hopes of an NFL career, with its glory and wealth, in favor of something more noble but much farther from the limelight. He joined the Navy. Eleven months later, he was a SEAL.

# CHAPTER 14

# Mateo's Last Dance

## 2011 Afghanistan

"We got this," said Gootz. From the looks of things, it would be straight out of the textbook, the same thing they had done a hundred times before. The compound was guarded by about twenty-five men, most of whom were inside. Their mission was simple. They were to do what they always did: go in, blow things up, get the bad guy or rescue the good guy, and then get out. The circumstances were odd, almost unimaginable, but an American diamond merchant and the captain of an oil tanker were being held hostage together. Likely, they would be in the basement of this mostly underground compound.

"We should just blow out the east side," said Jacobs. It wasn't the first time he had said it, and it still seemed a good idea, but their platoon leader, Slade, wouldn't allow it. "We've been through this. We don't know if our men are there, and I am not about to poke my head in and find out. We'll draw fire to that side, then you and Gootz are going to rain fire from the inside. Radio if our men aren't there, and you can take cover. Then we'll blow the place and come in through our new entrance. If you don't have a place for cover, or if our guys are there, radio and throw a grenade out the east window where we are fighting. We'll make sure to stay out of the way."

All six agreed.

Gootz and Jacobs took off like leopards, going through the trees with lightning speed and somehow avoiding every brown leaf and dry twig that could crack or make a sound. The enemy had cleared all shrubs and trees within a hundred yards of the compound, a distance Gootz could cover in less than fifteen seconds with all his gear. Jacobs would be right beside him. They made a quick evaluation of their target. There were two men near the door who were playing a game, unaware of the two of them secluded among the trees. So, 105 yards from the entrance, they sat silently in the darkness and waited.

*Tat-tat-tat!* All the men outside the compound turned their heads east as two of their own fell. A flurry of yells brought five men out of the barricade. One of the men who had been playing the game kept guard while his companion joined the firefight.

Gootz and Jacobs took off. Seconds later, they were against the west wall, back to back, headed towards the corner where their card-playing gunman was stationed. Gootz was facing the direction of attack. They hoped to get in the compound without a shot, but knifing the man was too risky. Gootz put his ten-inch blade away and kept his assault rifle in hand. He had two grenades ready at his knee. He nodded and knelt down, and Jacobs turned. They came around the corner at the same time, and two bullets were the fate of the man waiting at the door. Before he dropped, they kicked him away, and Gootz threw a fully cooked grenade into the doorway. It exploded before it hit the ground, and they ran in.

Two were dead, and they finished off one more who was still moving. After twenty-seven more bullets, another seven had died. Jacobs called to Slade, "Let it fly!" Seven seconds later, *Sssssssss PSHOOOO.* All the men outside the compound left this world, and the east wall was now the east door. Four SEALs ran in to meet their brothers.

Mullens had the best arm. He threw a grenade down the stairs and through the door on the right so that they could make their way down before the explosion. There were a few yelps, then a deafening *PSHOOOO.*

They all blazed in and cleared the room. They were nearly done. But the last room would be the most difficult.

They kicked the door down and got out of the way of any potential lead flying through the air. None came, but there were an unexpected ten men remaining. Four—two on each side of the hostages—had guns pointed at their captives' heads. There was only one door to the fifteen-by-fifteen room. This, too, was no new scenario. Slade pulled out a mirror and a pistol. He dropped two men causing pandemonium in the first line. Then the rest of the SEALs started shooting out all the lights in the basement. Slade shot out the light where the captives were.

Jacobs and Gootz already had their night vision goggles on. They ran in, spraying bullets, with the others right behind them. Gootz rushed towards the merchant, ended the lives of the captors, and put himself between the merchant and the rest of the party. Jacobs was right behind him, but the captain was wounded before Jacobs killed his man. The shot was in the arm, and, as far as they could tell in the dark, he seemed able to run.

They surrounded their liberated men and emerged as a whole, heading towards the stairs. Slade led the way with Jacobs and Gootz watching the rear. They went upstairs without a hitch and a few seconds later were exiting the building through the door where Gootz and Jacobs had entered.

It was only a mile and a half to their pickup. Each of the SEALs could have made it in less than nine and a half minutes, but the men they saved would lengthen it to about fifteen if they left them to their own feet. Instead, each freed man locked arms with two SEALs. This was excruciatingly painful for the captain, but his will to survive surmounted the pain, and he pushed through. It would only be twelve minutes locked up like this.

About eight minutes into their escape, they heard a *Sssssss*, Slade yelled, "Cover!" just before a rocket whizzed by them and blew up a tree beyond them. No one was hurt, and they took cover behind the newly fallen tree. Then gunfire started raining down on them. Their assailants were obviously unprepared for this battle and had started shooting a little too soon. Each SEAL donned his night vision goggles and resumed the work of death.

The gunfight lasted about ten minutes. Then they took off again and reached their pick-up point without another incident. The captain and Jacobs were swiftly pulled up the rope first. Then the merchant and Gootz started up. When they were about halfway up the rope, a single *TAT* was heard. Gootz let out a scream that was muffled in the merchant's chest. Slade immediately dropped Gootz's assailant, a straggler from the previous firefight. The rest made it up safely.

There was a lot of blood coming from Gootz's leg. His knee and thigh were in pain, but that was as far down as it went. He couldn't feel his foot, which was turning blue. Jacobs applied pressure, and, after twenty seconds he could feel a pulse in the ankle, so he opted not to tourniquet. "You're gonna be fine, Gootz. Just hang in there a little longer, and a surgeon will fix you up good." Gootz looked at him, nodded, and gritted his teeth. He wasn't faint from loss of blood; that had already been staunched. It was the pain in his leg that was more than he could handle, and he passed out.

# CHAPTER 15

# CHANGE OF PLANS FOR MATEO

---

### 2011+ Southern California

"The leg would have been useless for the rest of your life, Petty Officer. The blood supply was compromised, and you would never have had any feeling in the leg with that blown sciatic. Those two things combined meant that, down the road, it would have had to be removed, or you would have had problems more serious than the one you are currently dealing with. That's why we took the leg."

Those were the words of Mateo "Gootz" Gutierrez's surgeon. It was a hard pill to swallow for a young man who had sailed through high school and college to become a warrior at the highest level, largely because of his legs of steel, but he was alive and grateful.

"Thank you, sir," replied Mateo. "I very much appreciate you saving my life."

"And your country thanks you. The good news is that, these days, prostheses are very functional, and you will be able to get around just fine."

But getting around was the least of Mateo's worries. *Now what?* That was the real question. Very functional or not, a prosthesis was not going to allow him to remain a SEAL. His previous dreams of playing in the NFL were all but a memory. What was he going to do? How could anything live up to the superhero life he had been living? It seemed he had always been destined for greatness. How could he keep that up? He mused over these questions every day for the next week while he awaited his discharge. Perhaps he could become a police officer. As a former SEAL, he would be an ideal candidate for a SWAT leader. He could look at the FBI. Even without his former leg, he figured the physical demands would be a cakewalk after BUDS. He could join some high-profile security firm. All these ideas seemed good, but *what would be best?*

As he pondered these questions over and over, the time came for his exit interview and discharge. Going into the interview, he was not exactly sure what to expect. Mateo never wanted any praise for what he did, but he expected he would hear something like, "You served well," or "We all owe you a great deal." He wasn't let down.

But there was something else in the interview that surprised young Mateo. He felt like the admiral could somehow look into his soul, as if he could communicate on a higher, inhuman level. Mateo expected to just have a discussion and be let go, but that wasn't what happened. Mateo had been through BUDS, hell week, and numerous operations, but none of that prepared him for this. It certainly wasn't physically demanding to stand on the crutches, but it was mentally taxing. The way the officer could see into Mateo, the real Mateo who lived inside him, made him dreadfully uncomfortable, but it was a welcome intrusion, and he didn't fight it, hoping that he would get some insight into his future. In this, too, he was not let down.

"You are worried, Petty Officer," said the admiral, noticing the nervousness in Mateo's eyes.

"I don't understand, sir," replied Mateo, because he wanted more guidance.

"Yes, you do. You are worried that the rest of your life will not measure up."

Mateo wasn't sure how best to respond to the admiral's clairvoyance, but considering the admiral could see into his soul anyway, he saw no point in hiding anything. "I don't see how anything could measure up to the SEALs, sir."

The admiral's eyes penetrated Mateo with a confident assurance that helped him feel calmer. "The world may not measure up. The comradery, the discipline, the excitement. Those are gone."

Mateo's eyes started to water. He gritted his teeth, trying in vain to hide his sorrow.

"You, however, will always measure up, Petty Officer Gutierrez. You are a SEAL. You will stand for us back home. You will exemplify who we are. Every young man you know who dreams of becoming a SEAL will look up to you. What you do with that image is entirely up to you." The admiral paused to let the gravity of what he said sink into Mateo's heart.

Mateo had not considered this. The image of a Navy SEAL as seen by the people around him would be largely determined by Mateo. How he acted, and, more importantly, who he was would define what others thought of all SEALs. He did not want to let his brothers down.

The admiral continued: "But I know who you are. You will not let us down. The world may not measure up, but you will. And for all you know, the world may need your help again. Enjoy your life, Petty Officer."

There was a quick dismissal, and Mateo was sent to meet his parents. He was worried that when he arrived at John Wayne Airport and his parents saw him for the first time without a leg, his mother would break out in uncontrollable sobs. She did cry, but her embrace let Mateo know that any amount of pain she felt upon seeing her baby torn up like that was swallowed up by her pride for the man he was. The tearful smile on his father's now wrinkled face belied the same sentiments. Notwithstanding the life he was leaving behind as a SEAL, it was good to be home.

Mateo's parents had a thousand questions for him, and for the first fifteen minutes he did his best to answer without betraying his code of silence. During a reprieve in the onslaught of inquiries, he looked out the window to see the same buildings he grew up with pass by. Memories flooded his still turbulent mind as he saw all the places he had romped around in as a kid. He had obviously seen these during his tenure as a SEAL, but now they were to become a permanent fixture in his life. He was no longer a crazy kid. He was a man, a retired SEAL.

After a few minutes, the images all started blending together. His mind went back to the words: "The world may need your help again." *What did that mean?* Mateo didn't know, and he didn't think the admiral even knew, but whatever he did, he was going to make sure that if Mother America called again, he would be ready to answer.

FBI, CIA, NSA, LAPD, US Marshals—each had its own level of appeal, but Mateo decided that he would capitalize on the GI bill and go back to Southern California to finish his degree while he figured things out. When he enrolled, in true hero form, he decided to give back to his country—as if he had not already given enough—by starting a self-defense class for women on campus. Even before the semester started, word spread fast that a retired Navy SEAL was going to teach self-defense, and several men approached him to inquire if they could attend. Enrollment was so high that he *mostly* had to turn them down. He could only accommodate twenty-five women in his class, but he also needed five men who could act as assailants and dummies.

Teaching the class ended up being one of the best decisions of his life, because a beautiful young sophomore by the name of Mary Collins enrolled. She was smitten by Mateo's good looks, hard work, and concern for others. Her intelligence and humility matched her beauty, and eventually she would change her last name to Gutierrez.

It didn't take that long for Mateo to realize that having a resume with Navy SEAL on it was an excellent asset, no matter what field of work he chose. As long as there were people to work with—but most especially men—he would be able to capture an audience and immediately claim the respect of the those with whom he was engaging. He decided to put a few business and psychology classes on his schedule to test the waters.

Soon enough, he became a businessman, but it wasn't because of a few As on his transcript.

Like many of his SEAL brothers, Mateo stayed in shape even when he was not on the front lines. It hurt like hell, but because he made it a point to walk or jog every day and to go to the gym three times a week, in a few short months he was proficient at running again.

It was during his second semester that Ben Draper, a representative from PEN Health, a general nutrition and sports nutrition ingredient supplier, was at the school. He was on a two-day assignment to visit with and, potentially, interview students from the departments of exercise science, nutrition, and biology. His hope was to find potential sales representatives and new product formulators.

One of the stops he made was the gym. Although he was an avid cross-fitter, exercising was not on Ben's agenda. He was there to observe what was on the shelf for supplementation at the gym's nutrition store—just a quick check on trends for college-age consumers.

The gym had an indoor track that Mateo hit every day after he lifted. As it happened, Ben was leaving the gym when he looked through the large glass wall that separated him from the track. There he saw twenty-five or so young ladies and as many young men making their way around the last quarter of the track, but one stood out to him. His highly chiseled, tank-topped upper half was impressive, but the same was true for any number of athletes and other young men at a college gym. He was a little older than most of the others but didn't look quite old enough to be a professor, but that, too, wasn't noteworthy. What made Ben keep looking at this particular young man was his limp. He seemed too healthy and fit to have a limp.

Curiosity got the better part of good manners, and he was staring at Mateo as he approached. Mateo noticed, but it was not the first time, and he didn't pay Ben any mind. When Mateo was close enough that people started dispersing around the bend, Ben couldn't believe his eyes.

There was no leg from the knee down on Mateo's right side. He could also see that not only was he running on his prosthesis, he winced every time he stepped with that leg.

*Determination* was the first word that came to Ben's mind. He needed to speak with Mateo. He was curious about what accident or cancer had taken the leg but certainly had no plans to ask. He was far more interested in learning how determination and dedication had gotten this young man to the point that he was in extremely great shape and pushed himself to run in pain even without the full use of both legs.

There was only one exit from the locker room to the main area, which housed the nutrition store and a few restaurants, so Ben decided to watch and wait for the arrival of this intriguing individual. At a minimum, this was going to make an awesome motivational story he could use internally or with clients. Beyond that... who knew? That might be his next salesman.

After about thirty minutes of watching panting young people, water bottles, sweat, and gym bags, Ben saw Mateo emerge from the turnstile. He jumped up. "Young man... young man," he said as he drew closer to Mateo.

When Mateo realized that someone was trying to get his attention, he pulled out his earbuds, locked his eyes, and put on a smile. "Can I help you, sir?" he said.

*A gentleman. Very nice,* thought Ben. He put out his hand to shake and said, "I hate to be so impudent, but I couldn't help but notice that, on the track, you kept pushing yourself even though it was obviously quite painful. I also noticed that five percent body fat would be an extreme exaggeration on your account. I just had to ask: Why do you excel? What pushes you to? Most people would give up."

Mateo smiled slightly. Bragging was the last thing on his mind. "Oh, there must be others. I've always been in pretty good shape. The leg is a more recent development, but, in the long run, if I push myself, I don't think it will slow me down too much."

Ben liked his attitude. "So were you an athlete?"

"I played sports in high school. I even got a spot on the football team here, but that didn't last very long." Mateo laughed in a harmlessly deceptive way, leading Ben to think that he had gotten cut from the team.

"I hear ya. Been there, done that." Ben's laugh was sincere. He had gotten on the baseball team at his *alma mater* but never got any playing time. "Just out of curiosity, do you use any supplements, like whey protein or vitamins or anything?"

"Uh, yeah. I take a whey protein powder. I'm not trying to bulk up, but I think it helps with recovery."

*Perfect. This guy's already a believer. He can sell,* thought Ben. "I'm Ben, I don't think I got your name."

"Mateo."

"Mateo, huh? You don't by chance speak Spanish, do you?"

"I do, but not by chance."

Both laughed, and now Ben was even more interested.

"Well, look, Mateo. I'm a recruiter for a health food ingredient company. We don't have any of our own consumer brands currently, but we supply lots of other brands. In fact, the whey protein you take may very well be made by us. We're always looking for driven people to represent our company. Do you have any interest in sales?"

Mateo thought for a moment. Internally, he winced. *Salesman—how much more mundane could it get?* But another part of him went back to the admiral's words: *The world may need your help again.* Business had become more appealing as of late, but now he had an opportunity in front of him, the platter didn't seem as silver. He kept the smile on his face and nodded a little, saying, "Perhaps."

Ben's spirits were dampened at the lackluster reply, but he kept a facade of continued interest. Then he used his method for moving on from a potential job candidate who was in college. "Well, let me give you my card. Just send me your resume, and we'll be in touch."

Mateo's face acknowledged the brevity of his resume, but he also knew that he had a very special ace in the hole. "Well, it would be a pretty short resume."

The fact that Mateo didn't just end with "okay", along with his playfully mischievous smirk, let Ben know he really did have some interest but perhaps something was holding him back. "Have you never had a job?"

"Except for the brief stint to play football, for me it was pretty much high school, then Navy."

"Oh, what did you do there?"

"A lot of combat, a lot of traveling. I was a part of SEAL Team Five."

Ben lowered his head a little, looked at him, and said in an awed tone: "You're a Navy SEAL."

"Retired, sir, but yes, I am a SEAL."

A newfound respect showed in Ben's eyes, and he now understood why Mateo might be conflicted about taking a job in sales. "You must have some stories to tell."

"Not really, sir."

A look of mutual understanding passed on both their faces. "Fair enough, I thought that a young man such as yourself must have gotten into an accident—"

Mateo cut him off. "I'm sure that the bullet was no accident, sir."

Ben nodded again at Mateo. "We owe you," he said as he shook Mateo's hand again. "Well, I know there are a lot of things, probably much more exciting, you can do than work with us, but even though you won't be physically or mentally challenged in a way that even comes close to what you have experienced, sales is a good, very high-paying, high-travel job. If you have anything near the personality that I think you do, you will do very well, and we will take care of you and yours."

Mateo hung on every word. He took Ben's card, and they parted ways. His mind was moving quickly through different life scenarios. Maybe becoming a civilian in the civilian world wasn't such a bad idea after all. He knew of some other servicemen who'd had trouble finding or keeping good-paying jobs. So, he certainly didn't want to pass up a great offer.

Because physical training was no longer going to be part of his job, he would have to make a point to exercise regularly, but in the grand scheme of things, that seemed a small sacrifice. Besides, that is what he was already doing as a student. Furthermore, even though they still had not gotten married, Mary had started talking about children. In an instant, Mateo's mind even went forward to a time when he would have several children. Going to their school activities, sports, and other events was very appealing, something his father couldn't do until later in life. If the money really was there, he wouldn't have to work long hours or multiple jobs. He would probably work from home, and, except when he was traveling, he could spend time with his family and be a part of his kids' lives. What had started as an opportunity about which he was ambivalent had in a few quick moments become very interesting. He would definitely call Ben.

It ended up being a better opportunity than Mateo had originally thought. PEN Health was more than happy to accept his military service in lieu of a degree. He also found out that the pay was going to be $80 to $120K if his work met the average for the team. If he excelled, the sky was the limit. Over the course of a few phone calls, they all but offered Mateo the job, but proposed to have him officially start at the end of the school year so that he could take a few business classes in the meantime. This, of course, worked out perfectly. Now that he had employment secured, Mateo and Mary could plan a wedding.

A few years and one child into his new life, Mateo thought that, besides becoming a SEAL and marrying the most wonderful woman in the world, his sales job at PEN was the best decision he had ever made. He loved his job. He was able to travel enough that it was exciting, and he could take his wife on some trips, but he was home enough that he didn't get burned out. As he could make his own schedule, he taught morning and afternoon self-defense classes for women twice a week. After each self-defense class, he worked out. Unfortunately, he never lost his limp, but even with the limp he could easily run a sub-six mile for a 5k. And best of all, he crushed business averages and made in excess of $260K.

The money was money well earned. PEN Health was a very scientific company. They kept on file thousands of papers detailing the benefits or risks of some of the bigger ingredients like whey and soy protein, the standard vitamins, and common minerals. For new forms of vitamins or novel micronutrients and phytonutrients, they often funded the research themselves. The motto of their owner and founder, Janic Helms was "If it doesn't work, don't sell it." Using that paradigm, they only distributed ingredients that were strongly correlated with a health or performance benefit that was clinically reproducible. Though not a scientist himself, Mateo jumped into the literature headfirst. Every term he was unfamiliar with, he looked up. Every metabolic process or pathway that he had not seen before, he studied. Before long, he was convinced of the worthwhileness of the products he was selling and could talk about them to anyone, from the casual user to the biomedical researcher.

Most of what Mateo did involved making phone calls from home and visiting clients. However, one of the more exciting things that he did was attend trade shows. At national shows, PEN had a booth that took up a large 30' × 30' area. Most of the floor space was carpeted. Umbrellaed pillars showcased the various products they made or distributed, and under these pillars were small tables for meeting with prospective customers or small clients. The back third of the floor space was a covered area that ran along the aisle. The aisle face was covered with pictures of beautiful men playing basketball and beautiful women doing yoga and eating breakfast cereal to promote PEN's focus on health and active life-style. On the inside of the wall were two tables for larger meetings with clients. At the far end of this section were stairs that led to a mezzanine that had two meeting areas separated by a thin barrier.

The pictures and color schemes changed, but the bare bones were always the same, show after show and year after year. Mateo had seen it so many times, he made a bet with his co-worker that if the co-worker put a nickel anywhere on the booth and then described the location properly, he could find it in one attempt blindfolded. His buddy took him up on the offer, and Mateo ended up getting a free meal.

Working a booth was fun, but the real excitement lay in the energy surrounding a show. Thousands of people, very few of whom he knew, were there to start a business, find the next big thing, or strengthen current ties. Because of that, everyone was on their best behavior, and everyone wore a smile.

The nightlife was good, too. Mateo had plans every night to take clients to dinner. If it was a really big client, they would do something more spectacular. Once it was a comedy club; another time it was the Anaheim Angels. Whatever it was, they always had fun, and the best show of all was PFINE.

# CHAPTER 16

# FROM BROKEN TO FREEDOM

## 1990 Upstate New York

*Blake is a boy's name.* Little Blake Weathering had been teased about it every day of her early childhood. Although no one had no record of her birth name being Blake, it was nonetheless clear that that was her name. At one year old, or so the orphanage assumed, she was quietly dropped off at a fire station in Rochester, New York, without any papers and no information. About three days later, the blessed day arrived for the Weathering family to pick up their long-awaited baby girl. The situation had been explained to them, and they were more than happy to take the child on short notice.

It was the happiest and most exciting day of their life. They made the quick ride from Syracuse to Rochester, all the while trying to think of a name for the nameless baby. By the time they arrived, they had settled on either Heidi or Sylvia, but it wasn't to be.

They looked at the cute little girl, who could barely stand and was too shy to look them in the face. "Come here, sweetie, it's okay," coaxed Lucy.

"Hey, I brought something for you," said Jim in typical Dad style, trying to buy her affection. Understandably, she did not respond and stayed clinging to the leg of the foster mother who had watched over her for the previous few days.

A boy had arrived at the house that day who was currently rough-housing with another young boy and terrorizing all the little girls. His name was Blake. The foster mother yelled at him, "Blake, knock it off," and the little girl looked up.

Even without the slightest bit of motherhood on her resume, Lucy immediately noticed this. She asked, "Blake?"

The little girl looked up with large, sad eyes at the stranger.

"Is that your name? Is your name Blake?" Lucy implored.

The little girl kept a bead on the stranger's eyes. Lucy bent down, opened her arms, and said, "If that's your name, then that's what we'll call you. Can you come here and say hi, Blake?"

Blake put out her hand, took one step, and started to fall, but she was caught by her new mama, and they enjoyed the sweetest hug, one that would last a lifetime.

Eventually the teasing about having a boy's name tapered off. Unfortunately, it was supplanted by ridicule about being a nerd. Lucy had taught many things to her only daughter, but the one thing that was most instilled in her was a love for books. Until the time that she attended kindergarten, Lucy had a goal to read at least five books to her little girl every day, and she did.

The very first morning Blake woke up in her new home, Lucy met her with a smile, a cuddle, and a book. She got two more books before nap-time and two right before bed. It was a tradition that was never broken.

So, it was no surprise that little Blake would turn into the girl who always had her nose stuck in a book. The teasing hurt for a while, but when the subjects got deeper and the tests got harder, it was Blake who had the last laugh. While school presented a challenge to many students, most classes were an afterthought to Blake.

When she was thirteen, she decided to learn the piano. In six months, she was playing *The Entertainer* from memory, and at one and a half years in, she could sight-read most any hymn, heard or unheard, from the church the Weatherings attended. Soon after that, Blake grew bored with the piano and picked up clarinet even faster. Concurrently, when she started high school, she chose Spanish as her foreign language, and while most kids were still struggling to master about twenty irregular verbs, she had already finished *Don Quixote* and was able to do orientation for foreign students that came as part of the school's student exchange program with Peru.

Through work with the community college, Blake was able to graduate from high school a year early with some university credits already under her belt. The biggest drawback of having spent so much time in her books was that, except for homecoming, prom, and a few other group events, she didn't date any boys growing up. But when she got to full-time college, her heartstrings and hormones started pulling her attention more to the men who suddenly surrounded her. Indeed, she was a minnow among sharks.

By most standards, Blake was a pretty girl, and the older college guys took notice. She was first asked on a date only three weeks into school. Her mind was full of apprehension about accepting a date with someone she really did not know, but it turned out well. She met a lot of people and had a lot of fun. Unsurprisingly, things did not work out with her and her first date, but the friendships she made all stayed intact. Unfortunately, not all friends are worth keeping.

There was a young man by the name of Drew. Drew was not really a part of her new group of friends, but he was semi-friends with one of the other guys and sometimes tagged along with them when his real friends were unavailable. As luck would have it, Drew was there on Blake's first night with the gang, and he immediately noticed three things: she was pretty, she was young, and she was naive.

Over the course of the next month, Drew, though not particularly welcome or unwelcome, spent a lot of time with the gang and as much time around Blake as possible. A couple of the other girls tried to warn

Blake that Drew wasn't the best guy to start a relationship with, but none of them knew just how horrible he was.

Still only seventeen, Blake went to her first party only a month and a half into her freshman year. In addition to being her first party, it was also the first time that she had gone anywhere with Drew without the presence of her other friends. They had been there only a minute when Drew indicated he would step away and be right back. True to his word, he returned, and he had a couple drinks with him. Up to that point, Blake had never had alcohol, and at first she tried to decline, but between his persistence and her desire to fit in, she eventually succumbed. She liked the first glass of beer and she ended up having a few more.

Unbeknownst to her, Drew had offered her two drugs for the price of one. Into her beer, he had dropped a little tablet he and his frat brothers called *Nice and Easy*. Next to alcohol, it was the most popular date-rape drug on campus. Having both in her system, she had little chance of resisting anything, and on the ride home he took a detour to his apartment and had his way with her.

She woke up in her own apartment the next day with no recollection of ever leaving the party, coming home, and certainly not going to Drew's place. Even so, she knew what had happened. Her sore vagina and the blood on her panty liner told the sad tale of violation.

She cried. She called her mama. They cried together. It was the worst thing Blake could remember in her life. Lucy understood what peer pressure was like, and she tried to console her little girl, but Blake couldn't be comforted.

She wailed so loudly that women two floors up in the dorms could hear her. She would have felt bad enough about getting slightly drunk and very indisposed by the drug, but her sorrow didn't end there. It was her first introduction to sex, and she hadn't wanted it. She'd had no joy in it and couldn't remember a thing about it. What should have been a most memorable experience ended up being a horrible rape. Her mama consoled her in this, too, and tried to tell her that it was better to not remember something so vile.

She appreciated her mama's words, but she felt robbed at the most basic level. How could anyone have taken this from her? For years she had looked forward to this most wonderful experience with someone she cared for, that basic human desire to completely open your heart to and share your body with someone you love. She wanted that joyous memory to ever be with her. But all she would have to remember was shame, pain, and blood.

At her mother's counsel, Blake went to the university officials to describe what happened. When questioned, Drew claimed that Blake accepted his offer very willingly, and he lied about giving her any drug other than the alcohol which she had gladly consumed. At the end of the day, Drew got a light slap on the wrist and smiled every time he saw Blake on campus.

Torn mentally and physically, Blake considered violence. Thoughts of using a knife to redraw his demonic smile entered her head. Almost immediately, she realized that to nurse such fantasies would mean only that Drew had won again. She had been deceived, and now she was being mentally beaten by him. She took a very literal time-out and a few deep breaths, then said out loud, "You will not beat me again." She immediately dropped to the floor and managed to crank out one modified push-up. From that point on, she would not be owned by anyone, especially by any man.

The next time she saw Drew, she smiled at him. After this happened a few times, Drew thought maybe he had a chance. Perhaps somewhere in her subconscious, she remembered just how good he was, and now she wanted, or, rather, needed more.

When he next saw her walking ahead of him, he hurried up and gently grabbed her arm to speak with her. Before he finished saying her name, she started to caress his face and interrupted him.

In the kindest voice possible, she said, "If you ever so much as touch me again, I'll load your eyes with so much pepper spray that if you can convince any stupid girl to have sex with you, your kids' eyes will hurt. Then I'll use my foot to return the favor for my bloody genitals. If you even try to speak to me again, I will call the police." Then she smiled, continued her soft touch up the side of his face, grabbed a handful of hair, threw him to the side and continued on her walk. Drew never looked in her direction again.

Becoming her own champion was invigorating. Having grown up in a very traditional home with a mother who managed the household, she had always thought that she would grow up, get married, and follow in her mama's footsteps. In the back of her mind, she still wanted this, and if the right offer came along, she would have accepted, but her first encounter with men had been so bitter that she decided that even if Mr. Right was out there, she wasn't going to sit around and wait for him to come swooping in and take her breath away. Nor was she going to search him out on her own. She had gotten burned and rebounded strong. From now on, she was her own woman.

Regarding her rape, Drew wasn't the only thing that disappointed her. She was disgusted with the school. They knew he was lying, but because she'd had a few beers, her case was thrown out the window. Up to that point, academically, she was still undeclared, but thus far had been taking classes geared toward her original passion: literature. With the injustice she had been served dwelling in the back of her mind, she wanted a change of major so she could one day implement major change.

One day while running—something that, along with Jiu Jitsu, she'd taken up after being raped—she saw a recruitment poster for the FBI. It had four good-looking young people on it, and one of them was a woman. *What's your job at the FBI?* she mused as she stared hard at this blonde-haired beauty. Then she read the caption below: *Become a Special Agent.*

She looked back at the woman. *I can do that,* she thought. She saw that there was going to be a booth for the FBI at the career fair the next day. Most of her morning was tied up with classes, but she decided she would skip as many as she needed to talk to an FBI recruiter.

There was a fairly large crowd around the FBI booth compared to most others. There were two male representatives attending it, no women. Blake began to feel somewhat intimidated, but she told herself that she was a champion, not a victim, and her fears subsided.

"Yes, there are quite a few women special agents, both in the field and in leadership," responded the representative when Blake made her first inquiry.

Blake's courage swelled even more upon hearing this. "Sir, I am only seventeen years old. I finished high school a year early because I didn't want to waste any time getting on with my life. I know I have a great deal of school ahead of me, but I don't want to waste time any more now than I did then. What do I need to do to become a special agent?"

The recruiter didn't think much of these words. He'd heard rhetoric like this at every school he visited. This was, however, the first time someone who was only seventeen had been that bold with him. This told him that, if nothing else, she was precocious.

"Are you in good physical health?"

"I'm getting there. I just started running and I can easily run an eight-and-a-half-minute mile for three miles."

"You need to get under six and a half."

"I will."

"Do you have any language skills?"

"Moderately fluent in Spanish, but I am fully confident that I can learn faster than most."

The recruiter stared at Blake for a moment. He was impressed with her confidence. Having worked for the Bureau for some time, he knew that the most important skills were mental acuity, focus, and toughness.

He could see all three in her. Impressed, he nodded and told her what to do. "The vast majority of special agents are one of three things: accountants, attorneys, or IT specialists. If you are as serious about this as you are making yourself out to be, then..."

While he spoke, Blake's spirit flagged a little. *Does he think I'm superficial? Am I superficial?* she started to wonder. Then, almost in an instant, she told herself, *This is who you are. Don't let anyone convince you that you're fake.* Without missing a word, she was back in the conversation.

"...I suggest that you study accounting. When you graduate, apply to law school. Keep training, then apply when you get your JD. With good grades you will be a shoo-in. In the event that you don't get in, you will be prepared for an excellent-paying job."

Blake put out her hand and gave the recruiter her firmest handshake, after which she thanked him and did exactly what he said. She graduated a quick two and a half years later with an accounting degree. With her grades and charisma, she was accepted to Columbia, Cornell, and New York University law schools. She chose Columbia. During her first year of law school, she obtained her CFA, and no sooner had she graduated and turned twenty-three, she was appointed a special agent.

# Part III

# CHAPTER 17

# Chandra's Accomplices

## 2022 California

Help. The biggest challenge that Chandra had faced during his last year of undergraduate studies in India was figuring out who would help him. Recruiting Indians was off the table for a few reasons. One, too many Indians were fond of America and, like himself, wanted to study there. Two, he would never be able to get them into the country. He needed someone already there who could help him attack from within.

Cautiously, Chandra had done what anyone does when in need of information: he'd gone to the Internet. He'd been cautious because he was sure that the US government was scanning online traffic, and he suspected the Indian government might be as well. He knew that if his search terms made his plans for terror too overt, he might get caught. So instead of looking up words like *attack,* he started with more general concepts, such as *What's wrong with America.*

Finding anti-American blogs and websites wasn't difficult, and for a time he'd thought finding the assistance he was looking for would be easy. He was wrong. Most of the content was so blatantly radical that Chandra didn't bother wasting his time on it. He assumed one or more of the authors had to be undercover, and flirting with such websites could lead to his demise. Others were white supremacists, whom he did not dare take his dark skin near.

The most interesting and likely candidates had been groups that wore the facade of going back to the country's core principles but might in reality be at least semi-belligerent. Two stood out in particular: the Knights of the Republic, and Travesty. He'd made a point to go visit them when he got to America.

Once he was in the States, he found visiting them was quite inconvenient. During his first year, he wanted to reach out to these groups in person to get a sense of how they thought. It turned out that to do this, he would have to drive thousands of miles. Knights of the Republic and Travesty both had annual meetings during the year, and Chandra was determined to attend them. He definitely wasn't looking forward to the four days of driving per visit, and he was going to be very upset if he spent all that time in a car and all that money on gas and nothing came of it.

He made his first trip in May, right after the end of the school year. He headed to a meeting with Travesty in western Missouri. When he first got there, he excitedly shared his contact information with a couple of others, but he soon stopped all attempts to make new contacts or to learn any information from them. In his mind, his presence there was itself a travesty. He found out that they were not a facade at all. They were a group of young people who were actually trying to make a change. They spoke about the wretched state of affairs in the country, but instead of finding ways to cause pain and suffering, they were trying to figure out how to spread their ideals and get people to elect more effective and just officials. Chandra wanted to vomit. After thirty minutes, he went to his car and made the long trip home.

About one month later, he went to Wisconsin for a get-together with Knights of the Republic. This too proved to be not what he was expecting, but it was quite fruitful. A more appropriate name for the organization would have been Knight of the Republic. There was just one twenty-six-year-old man. Chandra didn't let on that he had dark intentions, but the knight, Joe Allen, was pretty vocal about his own.

Joe was much like the boy whom everyone knew in school and later regretted treating so poorly. He was teased because he wore sweatpants instead of jeans. He was ostracized because he told jokes that no one else thought were funny, or at least were willing to admit they thought were funny. Worst of all, he was banished to the periphery of adolescent society just because he didn't fit into, or was not allowed to fit into, any of cliques.

Being a loner, however, was not reason enough to become a terrorist. Joe had another problem. Chandra had not studied a day of medicine in his life, but he could tell that Joe had some mental health issues. Late in high school, Joe developed a mild form of schizophrenia/bipolar disorder. His case was minor enough that it went unnoticed for years. His parents were so busy working and trying to make ends meet that they didn't notice any changes. And since he didn't have any friends at school, anything he said that was off the wall was dismissed as something smart, weird kids say.

As time went on, Joe's condition worsened, but he was always able to function. He went to college, but his high intelligence mixed with occasional bouts of mania made school boring, so he quit after his freshman year. For the next year, he worked part-time and started a new form of study: the Internet.

Over the course of the next couple years, he had two epiphanies. One, his life was going nowhere. Two, he hated America. To be sure, he had been radicalized, but by whom no one could say. He was indeed a product of no one noticing when he'd needed help. Thus, everything he learned on the Internet was truth, and he visited only bellicose anti-American sites. Still, he would have remained harmless had someone not arrived in his life to instruct him in the ways of terror.

Thus, Joe had started his own website (which only he frequented) and, after a few years, met Chandra, who found Joe to be an invaluable asset. Chandra saw the potential in Joe to do almost anything that many others could only dream of, and because he was also "not all together," as some would say, no one would pay attention to any inflammatory language he might accidentally use regarding his hatred. He was gold.

About a week after Chandra met Joe, a second helper emerged. Chandra received a phone call from a guy named Melchior. Melchior had met Chandra back at Travesty, and they had exchanged numbers. Melchior had seen the displeasure that Chandra exhibited when he was at Travesty. The feelings were mutual.

Melchior, an Iraqi, had come to the States as a child during Desert Storm when his parents fled the country. At first he had loved America, and his parents had taught him almost every day how grateful he should be for his freedom.

However, after 9/11, people started treating him very differently. He no longer felt welcome. Like Joe, Melchior found being alone a little distressing, but not enough to make him hostile. That changed, however, on an ill-fated day when a man yelled out his car window, "For America," and shot both Melchior and his parents. Only Melchior survived.

From that point on, he started following every conspiracy theory he could find. He was convinced he had been lied to his whole life. First he'd been deceived by a nursing mother adorned in a red, white, and blue dress. What he once thought was altruistic was now imperialistic. What once seemed to be to a mission to save blood was now a mission to save oil. Where he once thought America tried to promote democracy and freedom, he now thought they were trying to keep Russia in check. Melchior was convinced that everything America did was driven by self-interest and that in no way did the US do good. He devoted his life to extremism and sought some grand design to inflict pain on America. Americans were his enemy, and thus he and Chandra became demonic friends.

Before the three of them got to work, Chandra set up a call. It would be the only time that all three would speak with each other. He needed to lay down some ground rules, then present his plan.

"First, no email. Only cell phone calls, and never more than one minute," said Chandra.

"How often are you going to contact us?" asked Melchior.

"Once a quarter, maybe. And you two will never meet. If somehow one of us gets caught, it is better that the rest of us don't have descriptions," he said.

"Understood," replied Joe.

"First, we just need to work. Get a job in a food factory. Become an expert on how to make the products. Once you know all the ins and outs, we will strike. It will be a bloodbath."

Melchior thought this seemed a little stupid and not nearly as grandiose as he had hoped. "You just want us to blow up a factory?" he asked, his voice full of disillusioned pathos.

Chandra didn't flinch at Melchior's ignorance. "You would not go to a stranger's house, look at the food in their refrigerator, and take something without knowing what was in it."

"What's your point?" asked Joe.

"That is exactly what you do every time you go to the grocery store," said Chandra. After a pause and no comment from either accomplice, he added, "What Americans eat doesn't come from a farm. It comes from a factory, and they don't know how it got there. We poison the food, they kill themselves."

Melchior almost started to salivate. "It's perfect."

Joe wasn't as sure. "How are we going to do it?"

"If there is anything I know, it is that Americans don't want to know how their food is made. Having been in a couple different production operations, I learned more than I could with any amount of study. That is why you have to work and get to know the processes. You will find the best way to do it. I know it."

"And what about you? Are we just going to do the dirty work while you sit back and relax?" asked Joe.

"I will attack the heart of food. I will let you know more details when we get closer. Until then, just work."

Next, Chandra made some assignments. Joe went to Oregon and Melchior to Utah. It was brilliant. In the end, each of them would have two jobs to do. And once each of them had finished both jobs, there was no way they could get caught.

# CHAPTER 18

# FRIEND OR FOE?

---

**2023 Davis, CA**

Chandra didn't consider school part of his plan. In fact, it was quite obvious early on that the object of food science training was to teach students how to protect people from potential problems with their food. Chandra felt studying food science was a complete waste of his time, but in order to stay completely off the radar of the federal government in a post-9/11 society, he adopted the facade of an exemplary student.

Chandra became well known in the department for being brilliant. He didn't need to brag about his grades. Envy did it for him. He was also known for being a loner. He had no friends at all. This was exactly the way he wanted it. He certainly did not want any American friends, and he saw no reason to befriend any of the other foreign students, considering friendship more of a nuisance than anything.

Rita White was also well known in the food science department. She was plenty smart, but that is not why she was well known. People knew her as friendly and genuine but weird. Like Chandra, she was working towards a PhD in food science. Notwithstanding this, she was about as granola as they come. She almost never wore make-up. Her top half was always covered by either a plain t-shirt or a flannel shirt. Below, she wore baggy jeans, overalls, or khaki shorts, depending on the season. Every day, she wore either canvas tennis shoes or sandals, and she often had henna-painted ankles, feet, and toes. In the coldest times of the year, she kept warm with an alpaca wool coat, and in the summer she wore a straw hat.

Although she seemed weird and dressed plain, try as she might to hide it, Rita was quite pretty. For as long as she could remember, guys had always passed her secret love notes or knocked on her door to get her attention. However, over the past couple of years, she had become more selective and dated seldom, preferring to focus on travel and her studies.

Rita's research was focused on the benefits of industrial organic farming and local agriculture. During her last two years of undergraduate studies, and every year since, she spent a month each summer in a developing nation helping the locals build sustainable food systems (not much different than the ones that they had been using for thousands of years) that would increase the productivity of their farms. She also spent time with several South American farmers to learn how they grew indigenous crops so that ancient technology could be brought to North America to potentially improve the American diet.

This was the Rita who was intrigued by Chandra, a quiet foreigner who was smart and worked hard. Rita found him to be quite nice-looking as well. Accordingly, she tried to make eyes at him when their paths crossed in the hallways and started saying hi whenever she found an opportunity. Chandra of course noticed, but he didn't respond. This, however, only strengthened Rita's resolve.

After about two months of this, Rita knew that she had to do something different, something a lot more dramatic. Aside from her clothes and her not wanting to work for a large food company, people thought she was weird for being direct. There was nothing artificial about her, and she never beat around the bush.

Chandra never studied academics in his studio. The studio was where he made his plans, did his artwork, ate, and slept. Nonetheless, despite his brilliance, he did need to study to maintain his 4.0 GPA and keep receiving his income from the Indian government. In the basement of the food science building was a lab where he worked for his advisor. It had no windows and was a little dank, which meant that students didn't like being there. It was too gloomy for them but perfect for Chandra. That is where he always studied for school.

Like any other day, Chandra was at his desk when he heard the door to the lab open when there was no upcoming class. This was not common but not terribly singular, either, so he did not think much about it, nor did he make any attempt to see who it was. Then a girl with straight brown hair put her face right in front of his computer monitor so that they were now almost touching nose to nose.

"Chandra?" she prompted.

Chandra was upset that she knew his name and even more annoyed that she was speaking to him. He pushed back his chair to distance himself from her.

She followed him. "Why are you trying to get away from me, Chandra?"

He had no choice but to answer, "You don't know me."

"But I want to."

"No, you don't," he said as he moved his head as if to look around her at his monitor.

"I'll be the judge of that," she said as she stood up straight. "I want you to take a walk with me."

"No."

"Fine, have lunch with me."

"No."

"Dinner?"

"No."

Most people would have given up by this time, but Rita was not even fazed. It was refreshing. She had never been turned down by a guy before. This would be a challenge. It was fun. "Well, you do eat, don't you?"

"Yes."

"Good, glad to see you know *that* word."

Chandra was a little perturbed that he had given way with his last comment. "Well, I guess you should get going. I have some studying to do."

"Yes, I do need to get going," she said as she smiled and left.

The very next day, at 12:00 p.m. sharp, Rita showed up at the exact same place. Like last time, Chandra didn't look when he heard the door open. He certainly did not expect Rita again. He figured after the way he had treated her the day before, he would never have to worry about seeing her again, but he was very wrong. Before he realized it, she was in front of him with a smile and a burrito wrapped in aluminum foil. "Did you miss me?"

With as little expression on his face as he could allow while moving his mouth, he replied, "No."

"There you go with that word again," she said as she crouched down and put her hands on his shoulders. "You said you eat. I brought you something. It's bean and cheese."

As much as Chandra hated Americans and the thought of an American befriending him, deep down he did like the attention, and he was, after all, a heterosexual male. Even so, he definitely would not show any interest or pleasure. He gently pushed her to the side, then recommended staring at the screen. "I already ate."

"I don't believe you," she said.

Unlike his previous responses, Chandra did show a little emotion with his next response. A quasi-mischievous and quasi-sarcastic smile inched its way onto his face with smug complacency. Without making eye contact, he replied, "That's because I'm lying to you. Go away."

That one did hurt. She had never experienced rudeness like that before from anyone in her life. But she didn't let on that she was hurt. She just smiled, patted Chandra on the leg, and while opening her burrito said, "Well, I'm not going away. I am going to just sit here and eat until you eat with me."

"You will be waiting for a long time," he replied.

"I've got a lot of time on my hands." So, Rita sat there for an hour, occasionally making one-way conversation and less frequently getting the response, "You don't know me." At one o'clock, she had a 600-level statistics course she needed to attend, and so she left. *Good riddance*, thought Chandra. Surely that would be the last time that he would need to deal with her. His bad rubbish, however, kept returning—every day, with food.

After about a month, Chandra found himself in a very complicated and difficult situation. After the first two weeks of bringing lunch, she upped her game and started bringing dinner as well, meaning that he had to see her twice every day. Leaving school was not really an option, and going to another room meant being around more loathsome Americans, so he could not do that, either. Getting rid of her by using really vulgar language or bursting out into a screaming fit would jeopardize his school status and potentially his real mission.

Those were problems and conflicts caused by her presence, but there was one more that was of far more importance and complexity. He was starting to not only become inured to her presence but enjoy it. He absolutely could not become attached to any American. It would change everything. He had to distance himself. He had already begun to see that not everyone in America was a cannibalistic whoremonger. Every smile, every hello, every "What's up" angered him. He was angry because he had plans to make everyone hurt. But not everyone was bad. In fact, he had not met a single bad person in the US besides Joe and Melchior. It was for that very reason that he'd started spending all his time in the basement. He didn't want to see the good in anyone.

Then she had come. Not only was she good, but she was good-looking and kind of funny. *What is her interest in me, anyway?* he wondered.

Unaffected by any amount of neglect, she just kept coming back. He had to try something else. He knew that she could be the death of him and all his devilish plans.

With all these complexities on his mind, one day Chandra stopped working, turned, and looked her right in the eyes. Rita had to brace herself a little. It was the first intentional eye contact that Chandra had made. She was sitting on the floor against a piling that held up the three floors of the building they were under. As he folded his arms with a stare that now showed discontent, the most emotion he had ever given her, there was more stress in the air between them than in the concrete piling behind Rita's back. Then he spoke frankly. "What do I need to do to get rid of you?"

In a show of strength, she stood up and folded her own arms. She looked down at him in his chair, matched his intensity, and said, "Go on a walk with me. The first thing I asked you."

"You don't know me. How do you know I won't hurt you or rape you or something?"

*Baloney,* thought Rita. She called his bluff and took a chance of her own. "It's not rape if I agree to it."

A blast of emotion hit Chandra and sent jolts through his body like being drenched in ice-cold water. He wished he could have been angry, but something deeper, more fundamental overrode it. The mere mention of potential intimacy thrilled him beyond measure. He had no intentions of a relationship, but the male part of him wanted to leap at her, touch her beautiful skin, and kiss her face. He tried to hide it, but she could see right through his Saran-wrap facade.

He knew he was beat; he couldn't say anything without choking up a little now and getting caught in his fraud. He turned back to his computer, excited, angry, happy, and nervous all at the same time. Without saying a word and without looking at the food, he took a piece of naan that, like so many other items, had been placed beside him, dipped it in some hummus, and ate it.

The next day, at 12:15 sharp, just as she had on the previous four Thursdays, Rita arrived with a bag of food and a smile. This time, however, Chandra was not sitting at his desk. He was standing, facing the door in anticipation of her arrival, with a bright smile on his face. Reaching deep for the charm he had learned from Kalini and had used when he was accepted at the university, he bowed and said, "Are you ready to go for a walk?"

Rita thought that the hummus gesture had meant something, but she never could have imagined such a change as this. Either he really wanted to get rid of her once and for all, or she really was in grave danger of getting raped, but she was intrepid notwithstanding. She brought the sides of her mouth even higher and came in close beside him, wrapped her arm under his, and said, "I've been waiting for this moment for a long time."

By the time they were at the top of the stairs and ready to go outside, their arms were no longer tangled, but the onlookers could tell that they were being quite friendly with each other. Thus, the rumors began to circulate that Rita had a boyfriend in Chandra. Of course, no one believed it until they saw the two of them together themselves, which wasn't too difficult to arrange because Chandra was eating lunch and dinner with her every day for a week, and most every day after that.

But on this day, they postponed lunch and the two of them stepped outside. An October breeze kept them comfortable as the bright California sunshine blanketed them and everything within 150 miles. Rita had so many things to ask Chandra, some of which she already had asked but had received no response. Now she figured she had a chance, but she was not the first to speak.

"Why do you want to walk with me so much?"

"Because I like you," she said as a matter of fact.

In a most pleasant manner, Chandra replied, "You cannot like me. You don't even know me."

With an equally kind demeanor and with a sort of English no longer spoken in the US, she countered, "It is precisely for that reason that I do like you. I like everyone that I have no reason to dislike. And besides, I really don't dislike anybody unless they are a terrible person."

Chandra was a terrible person, but she didn't know that. Keeping a smile on his face, he shook his head in a disbelieving, disagreeing manner to convince her he was a terrible person without disclosing his plans. "I am quite sure I gave you plenty of reasons to dislike me. I ignored you. I insulted you. I pushed you away physically. I told you to leave. I even tried threatening you. Nothing worked. Why do you still like me?"

Rita stopped walking and they faced each other. "You were doing and saying things to get rid of me. Sometimes it hurt, but until I get to know who you actually are, I will continue to like you. I won't give up until I know you."

Chandra dropped the smile, his face serious. "You don't know me. If you did, you would not like me."

"I'll be the judge of that," was her response.

Chandra donned his smile again and nodded, and they kept walking.

Rita knew the whole exchange was fake. The language, the smiles, they were all superficial, but it didn't matter. It was the person inside she was after. She knew he could be completely rude one minute and disturbingly well-mannered the next, but neither of them was the real Chandra. He certainly could not be both, and she assumed he was neither, but what he was she did not know.

# CHAPTER 19

# LOVE AND SANITY

**2023–2024 Davis, CA**

Days and weeks passed with cordial friendship and meal dates, and before he knew it, Chandra Sandeep had acquired an emotional attachment to the pretty young American girl who wore overalls. This presented a huge, complicated problem for Chandra. If he were to be the dagger that would cut into the heart of America to repay the debts of his murdered family and others he met along the way, Rita was the shield that would prevent him. The problem was that he liked her—no, he loved her, very much. Every day he told himself he would not spend time with her and he would not eat with her, but every day he proved himself wrong. She was getting inside. She had penetrated deeper into his mind than any person had since Kalini, and what made matters worse was that he was relieved to have someone become a part of him because he had walked the lonely road for far too long. Internally, he had to put up safeguards so that she could not perceive his darkest and vilest thoughts, but he did not know how long this could go on. Still, he did not want to go on without her.

Unfortunately, Rita's heart also was starting to knit itself to Chandra. She was not so blind that she couldn't see that he was hiding things, but considering how long it had taken for him just to take that first walk, she didn't think much of it. Every day, she tried harder and harder to delve a little farther into the network that made up his mind. But he kept sending her on detours. If she could have gotten a little farther, she undoubtedly would have run for her life, but his cunning and his burgeoning love kept her around

They spoke about everything from tiles on roofs to types of dogs they liked, but because they were both in the food science department, and because they both for very different reasons had great interest in food, food was often the topic of conversation. After a month of eating whatever one or the other brought, they took things to the next level and started cooking together in a prep kitchen located in the basement of the department. Very soon, this became the most exciting part of the day for both of them.

Their hearts were not their only parts starting to yearn to be together. The erotic emotions of the two were in torrential turmoil. Though not sincere, Rita's quick response to Chandra's rape inquiry was always in the back of his mind. He found her physically gorgeous and mentally beautiful. Likewise, Rita thought his mocha skin and well-set nose were lovely in their own right, but she found his extreme intelligence and mysterious demeanor even more attractive.

During the first month of cooking together, Rita made several attempts at flirtation: a bump with the hip here, a caress of the arm there. Chandra countered on occasion but never made any attempts to start something. Furthermore, she made several offers to have him come over to her apartment, all of which were turned down. This made her heart sink and his heart ache. They both wanted to know each other better at all levels, but Chandra would not allow it. Over time, Rita became resigned to the idea of just having a friend, but deep down she longed for more.

After his fishing excursion, Chandra had sworn he would never eat another fish so long as he lived, and since he and Rita were both vegetarians who loved curry no matter what country it was from, finding meals they both liked was easy. They kept a bag of jasmine rice in one of the cupboards. The refrigerator, usually empty but always running, was where they kept their assortment of curry pastes. Coconut milk was kept next to the stove. Everything else was improvised. Chickpeas were common, but rarely did they repeat meals. Indeed, they were quite the envy of other students eating peanut butter and jelly, but no one joined them: either they didn't like Chandra already, or they found him unwelcoming when they did pop their heads in.

On a very typical day, while Rita was chopping bamboo shoots and Chandra was dicing onions and tomatoes, he did something very atypical: he started a conversation. Without making any attempts at eye contact and never breaking stride with his onion, he asked, "Why are you in food science?"

Rita had a puzzled look on her face when she answered. She was half puzzled that he hadn't gleaned the answer from their previous conversations and half puzzled that he would ask a thought-provoking question. "I love food, you know that," she began as she motioned to her handiwork, "and I want to make sure poor people have enough to eat."

"You don't fit in here. You are different," he said. And with that, Chandra was ready to end the conversation, but Rita wasn't. She wanted to know more. Even though months had passed and her love for him was growing, in many ways, he was still a stranger. She wanted to know him on a deeper level, but he never opened up. After a brief moment of reflection, she tilted her head and decided to try the virtue of a bargain. "You're right. There is more to my story, and I will share it with you if you give me more of your story."

Chandra kept a straight face, but inside, his mental lips were quivering. In his mind, he broke down crying and told her everything of his past: the loss, the death, the torture. She would hold him and wipe away his tears. She would get him out of the prison he was in.

Chandra knew he couldn't do that, but he wanted...he needed to know more about her. So, straight-faced, he stared back at her and said, "Agreed"—knowing that he would divulge very little to her.

Rita's face lit up. This was her chance, maybe her only chance. She stopped what she was doing, locked eyes with Chandra from across the table, and started by saying, "I didn't always wear straw hats and overalls."

"Okay," said Chandra, wondering what her clothing had to do with the story.

"Growing up, I was a brat," she said quite matter-of-factly.

Chandra cast her a doubtful look. The girl he knew was definitely not the "brat" type. *She's exaggerating,* he thought.

"I know you think I'm lying, but I'm not. I was the rich attorney's little girl who was spoiled with everything she wanted. I always wore the cutest skirts, always had the nicest, hottest new shoes, always sported the best hair and highlights and to show it off, I modeled on the side."

It was when she said she modeled that Chandra believed her. She didn't know it, but Chandra had seen her in fancy shoes and a gorgeous dress. Little did she know, she was wearing it in his portfolio.

"When I was fifteen, I got a brand-new BMW M3." Even though she had convinced him, Chandra shot her another incredulous raised eyebrow. "I took my friends out in it every night I wasn't on a date. And I was on lots of dates."

Chandra knew she didn't date anyone at the university except perhaps for him. Nonetheless, he could feel his blood pressure rise, thinking of Rita with some other guy.

"In fact, it was on a date that things changed for me. I remember it like it was yesterday. I was with a very good-looking guy. He was a friend of the family. He was rich, too. People thought we were a perfect match, and frankly, for the person I was then, he was a perfect match.

"We were cruising down Main Street, in my car that I had gotten detailed that day. There on the side of the road I saw a homeless man everyone called Crazy Frank, who lived under the overpass. My date yelled at him, 'Why don't you get a job, loser!' Then he said to me, 'What a lowlife. Always looking for a handout.'

"I didn't know what to think, I didn't know what to say. I just looked at the man pushing a shopping cart that contained all his earthly possessions. I looked at the sparkling manicure on my fingers holding the leather steering wheel. I looked at my two-hundred-dollar designer skirt I had bought for that night. I pushed my head back and heard my perfectly set hair crunch against the heated leather headrest. Everything seemed wrong."

Chandra knew where she was going. This story did not make things easier for him. Learning more about the one person on this planet that he cared about was both alluring and provocative. He wished he had never asked.

She was already a thorn in his side. She was both wonderful and American—two qualities he'd thought were mutually exclusive. She was proving him wrong. She was a potent example of the good in America, and he hated it, yet he loved her.

How he wished he had never met her, yet at the same time he longed to know her more. How he wished he was a bigger part of her life and she of his. How he wished he could love her at every level—but doing that would mean throwing away all his plans and abandoning those he had lost. And thus he was torn, wanting to hear more and wishing she were gone.

"That was it. I sold my car and donated all the money. I started shopping at the farmers' market. I started buying secondhand clothes. I started traveling to third world countries to volunteer, and I have never looked back.

"Over time, I realized that donations were great and necessary, but in many parts of the world, very few people have money, giving money to them does little. Helping people help themselves, on the other hand, always has a positive impact regardless of the monetary climate. So I settled on food because if people don't first have something to eat, they will not only be hungry, they won't have the strength to do any other necessary tasks of life, and their situation will only get worse. And that is why I am in food science."

Without an ounce of dubiety on his face and still no eye contact, he said, "You like real food, not the stuff in boxes. And let's be honest, if you set up some 'positive impact'"—Chandra made air quotes—"in a less developed country, in the long term some big business would come in, use fancy words, throw around a lot of money, and destroy any chances of sustainability. If you don't believe me, I've got one word for you: *quinoa*."

Rita thought for a second before speaking. When she had the gist of it in her mind, she let the words flow. "I agree that there is plenty of bad food out there in packages, but not all of it is bad. Sure, I like to prepare a lot of things myself, but we don't live in a world full of two-parent families with a spouse who stays at home, makes a trip to the farm every other day, and makes all meals from scratch. People don't have time to cook anymore. They need to be wise with their food choices. Like it or not, this is the world we live in. And as far as quinoa goes, just because someone else might destroy what I have worked to create does not mean that I should just give up."

Chandra's mind was in turmoil. He hated that he agreed that she was at least partially right. He hated that he knew more about her, and he hated himself for letting her pull his heartstrings. In his anger, he ended up blurting out, "It's all bad, and you know it." He felt dumb after saying it but just let it go.

Rita was quick to reply. "What about that curry paste in the fridge? The stuff we've been eating for the past month?"

Chandra didn't like to be put in his place. He also did not like the idea that he had helped support the very thing he was trying to say was vile. He had spent so much time deciding on the easiest way to break down the food system that he had completely overlooked the good in it. Thoughts of bread, healthy frozen entrees, and kids smiling while they ate ice cream started to creep into his head, but he had to shove them back out. He couldn't allow such nonsense to soften him. He had to keep his resolve, and he hoped the conversation would end there.

Chandra should have known that Rita would not let him out of their agreement. She had given him her story. It was now time for him to pay in kind. With all the seriousness and concern her eyes could muster, she looked at him and said, "Now tell me about you."

Chandra responded, "You don't want to know me."

"Yes, I do, and you promised. Please don't break my already aching heart."

It was the perfect moment for Chandra to finally get rid of her, as he'd tried to do for the first month of their acquaintance. He could end it now. But those words were too painful to hear. He couldn't break her heart.

Chandra took a deep breath. "I had a family once. A sister, a mother, a father. They all died." Overcome with sorrow and all sorts of emotion, Chandra stopped.

Just from the look in his eyes, Rita could tell he wasn't going to speak any more on the topic, but she was not done. She thought maybe he was starting to open up. All he needed was a little more prying and she could know who he was. She put her knife down and made her way to his side of the table. Chandra was bent over the stainless-steel counter, still cutting onions. She could see some water in his eyes, but she knew better than to ask whether he was sad or just responding to the onions. She slipped her arm in front of him, and he instinctively stepped back. She put herself between him and the table, then embraced him with all her love while asking, "When are you going to let me in?"

Chandra's heart was pumping like a locomotive as he furtively handled the knife in his left hand. He knew he could end this. One quick thrust of the knife right to the heart. Then he would not have to see her anymore. Then he would be free of his misery. Then he would not have to maintain this dual personality. It would be over. Not that he would actually have ended her life—he could never do that. The thought of anything hurting her was more than he could bear. He would do everything in his power to see that she was unaffected by his plans, and perhaps the only way to do that would be to end his own life. It seemed now or never.

He could just as well have been cutting bread and the tears would have rolled down his cheeks just the same. He gently hugged her back, his left hand trembling, and said, "You don't know me."

"I want to."

"No, you don't."

Rita, now crying herself, was disappointed and upset. How long would he do this? She buried her face in his chest and wiped her eyes. Then, she stopped hugging him and went back to cutting vegetables. Her melancholy face exuded the gravity of what was on her mind. She had to make a decision. She needed to either loose her heart from him forever or eternally tie it to his. She had had every reason in the world to say goodbye to him. Any person in their right mind would have left long ago. But a mind in love is often not right.

She cut a few more bamboo shoots into pieces and thought about the time she had spent with him. It was the most difficult thing she had ever done, and yet he was the thing she wanted most. She could not let him go. Being apart would be more heartbreaking than death. So, with her renewed resolve, half a smile came on her face, and she continued preparing lunch.

They ate and Chandra was hoping everything was back to normal. But things would never go back to normal. That evening, she started a new tradition: she accompanied him home on her bike. He begged her to leave, but she wouldn't.

When he opened the door, Rita saw the bare room with an easel where Chandra had been drawing something. "You never told me you do artwork."

Chandra was immediately filled with terror. That was off limits.

"No, that's just how I grade papers. I like to do it standing up."

Rita accepted the answer but felt he wasn't being completely honest.

Rita turned and went away. Chandra hoped that she would never visit his house again, but he immediately folded up the easel anyway. Unfortunately for both of them, it was not her last trip to Chandra's home.

# CHAPTER 20

# Eureka

---

**2023–2024 Hillsboro, OR**

J oe moved to Oregon. It was not quite clear what he would do yet, but he and Chandra had decided if he got work, they could figure things out later. They only knew that it would be best to move somewhere where people did not know him. Somewhere he could be a loner. Somewhere family would not pop in to check on him. Somewhere he could carry out evil in the privacy of his own home.

Though the plans were still germinating, given the amount of milk consumed in the US, and worldwide for that matter, a dairy seemed like a pretty safe bet. More or less randomly, they chose Willamette Pure in Hillsboro, Oregon as their target.

Unbeknownst to them, Willamette Pure's quality and safety standards were high, exceeding the requirements of the FDA's Pasteurized Milk Ordinance at nearly every point. Every dairy that sent them milk, whether it would be sold under the Willamette Pure label or not, had biweekly contact from the herd veterinarian regarding the status of the herd and segregation of all sick animals. They required that the raw milk sent to them be no more than 38ºF. Once raw milk was received, it was further cooled to 35ºF.

Their state-of-the-art facility had two lines for thermal processing of milk. And though the facility was state-of-the-art, the technology employed was nothing new. Line one was set up to do either high-temperature, short-time (HTST) pasteurization or ultra pasteurization/ultra-high temperature pasteurization (UHT). The second line only did ultrapasteurization.

Willamette Pure's HTST milk had about a fourteen-day shelf life. They put ninety days on the UHT milk, but in reality it could last much longer if not opened. From a microbiological standpoint, the UHT milk was one of the safest foods a person could consume. But Willamette Pure did not stop there in their commitment to safety. The real reason they were so state-of-the-art lay in their quality assurance and control.

Every part of the machinery that did not get sterilized daily was subject to at least weekly swabbing to ensure adequate cleaning and no growth of any aerobic (oxygen-based) microorganisms. They also did occasional anaerobic swabs to test for heat-resistant spores. All dry ingredients used in flavored products were required to have a certificate of analysis detailing the incoming microbiological load, or, in other words, the number of microorganisms present before they processed it.

Before employees could enter the production floor, they had to pass through a high-speed air chamber to blow off lint and dust. The tunnel terminal opened onto a room that had two hand-washing stations and one turnstile. The turnstile let only one person through per hand-wash. Inside the plant, Willamette Pure allowed only one type of footwear: steel-toed rubber boots with Bactostat, a nontoxic antibacterial resin, embedded in the soles.

Finally, they staffed one more person for quality control than most other dairies did. The production employees affectionately called this person "the watcher." The watcher's job was just to walk around and make sure that nothing appeared to be unsanitary or even just out of the ordinary.

Banners were posted on the walls with a saying: "Prevent the impossible." It was management's mantra, and the employees lived by it. Even though pasteurization would keep people from getting sick if *Escherichia coli* or another pathogenic microorganism entered the raw milk, they had to prevent contamination. Even though a little dirt in the mixing kettle wouldn't hurt anyone, they had to prevent contamination.

This they did, and their hard work didn't go unnoticed. They were the second dairy west of the Rocky Mountains to receive a third-party "Stellar" rating for a Global Food Safety Initiative audit. They were the recipient of the 2008 *Safe Food* magazine Safe Plant Award. And most recently, they were chosen by the USDA and the Oregon and Washington departments of agriculture and education as a major supplier for the USDA's school and daycare food program. And so, the work clock never stopped at Willamette Pure. Whether it was production or cleaning, there was always work to be done. In many ways, Willamette Pure had the safest milk in the country, perhaps even the world, and it seemed that nothing could go wrong with their product. Like the banners said: "Prevent the Impossible."

In summer 2023, they hired Joe.

After a quick inquiry into the hiring process, Joe learned that all initial hires had to first complete six months working as temporary employees. The temp agency of choice for Willamette Pure was Temps for Less, located in the same town. He put in his application, told them of his desire to work at Willamette Pure, and waited.

It became pretty apparent that he was not going to get hired anytime soon, so in the meantime he applied to other dairies in the West and worked at a restaurant bussing tables so that he would have enough money to stay off the streets. It would take him a full six months and a great deal of mental anguish inflicted by Chandra before he got the call to come aboard Willamette Pure.

He started work in the palletizing area. All palletization was automated, so usually it was a pretty easy job. He kept the area clean and moved the pallets of finished milk to temporary cold storage to await pickup for distribution. There were inevitably problems, and he would occasionally need to hand-stack things, but as a general rule the process went pretty well. This is what Joe did his first several months at Willamette Pure.

Even though he was stationed in one spot, Joe became familiar with the plant. Chandra promised him there would be spots of vulnerability, but as far as Joe could tell, the system was bulletproof. The fillers were all enclosed and would stop if opened. While the product was being processed, it was in watertight piping and equipment that maintained pressure so that if a leak did spring, it would not allow outside penetration. And if that were not enough, the containers were tamper-evident.

It seemed to Joe that the best and probably only spot for mischief was at the beginning of the process: either the batching station where beverages such as chocolate milk were mixed, or one of the tanks that held the recently batched products that were awaiting pasteurization. The batching station seemed the more likely of the two, as it was where almost all the ingredients were added and it was often a low-supervision job for one person. Joe felt pretty confident that the batching station would be the target if he could get a spot there. The problem was that getting a spot there was no easy task. It was the second highest non-supervisory job in the plant, and there were a few with seniority already on the list to take the next available opening.

Willamette Pure had a policy that after six months of employment, new hires were to rotate among different areas of the factory in two-month increments so that they could put in a bid for the job they would like best. After a few transfers, Joe made it to the batching area. What he assumed would amount to mixing a glass of chocolate milk turned out to entail fifty-pound bags, pulled muscles, and sweat, some of which made its way into the milk. Nonetheless, it seemed like the perfect spot to do his handiwork, so he worked especially hard with the hope that he might get hired there, even if only as a helper.

Handling the ingredients also afforded him a much greater understanding of the composition of the products. At first, he just opened the bags and dumped their contents in, but considering that knowing the function of the ingredients might prove useful later, he started asking questions and doing what he had done for years: looking things up online. For instance, a white thickening powder called carrageenan was a naturally sulfated polysaccharide extract of red seaweed used to impart viscosity, suspend particles—especially cocoa—and emulsify. He found out that there had been some recent debate about the safety of carrageenan, with some researchers affirming its propensity to cause ulcers and cancer while other researchers were asserting that no such effects occur when food grade carrageenan is used and further claiming it might even reduce cancer risk. It was tough to tell who was right. Joe found that ingredients can be controversial to say the least.

After Joe had assisted the batcher for a month, they had an order to work on some juice. Apparently, one of their customers was in a pinch because the co-packer that normally handled their juice products was temporarily offline due to a fire. Even though Willamette Pure was not in the juice business, they were approved to process juice, and they did have the right filler for the customer's package, so they agreed to help the customer fulfill their demand.

Joe saw the packages in the filling room. They read Kiddos Juice, 50% less sugar than regular juice. *Wow, I wonder what sort of chemical they add to the juice to make it lose half its sugar*, Joe thought.

As his distorted yet intelligent mind mused over the matter, he started doing some math and figured it out. There was no secret ingredient to reduce sugar; it was just more water. Double, to be exact. When the pump had finished putting in the necessary water to get started, Joe went back to assisting the blender. In his mind, he was having a good laugh about the product: apple juice with half the apples, *I guess we just really like convenience, don't even have to add water yourself!*

After work, he went to the grocery store to look at other products on the shelf. Indeed he was right. People shopped for convenience. From pre-sliced apples to pre-popped popcorn to pre-made peanut butter and jelly sandwiches with the crust removed eating was made as work-free as possible. This was definitely going to make his job easier.

What wasn't going to make his job easier was the waiting list for the batching area. There was no doubt in his mind that a promotion to batcher was his best bet. That is where the ingredients were added and, realistically, the only open spot in the entire process. If he couldn't get a spot there, the only thing he could do would be to try to sneak into the batching room at some point, which wouldn't be easy. Product was actually in the blender only for short intervals, and bringing in the needed quantity of his ingredient would be difficult. In the meantime, his plan was to watch for patterns and openings to get his work done. He would have only one shot.

Or so he thought. His next training stop was prep. He wasn't sure how he could have overlooked this. Prep was in the back of the plant. He was often there by himself. Since the only machine he needed to know to operate was a scale, it was the lowest-tech position in the plant. As such, it also paid the least. In other words, it was a job no one wanted. This was it.

It was simple. The job entailed pre-weighing ingredients that the blenders then put into the batch. For large items such as sugar or cocoa, most of what the blenders added was full bags. Smaller items like vitamins, minerals, salts, and stabilizers—or, for Joe, poisons—were weighed and then put in small bags, upon which he wrote weights and lot numbers.

The work he did in the blending room and on his computer allowed him to know which ingredients would be the best candidates for substitution. Replacing a bag of stabilizer would be too obvious, but the salts, vitamins, or minerals would be a different story. With the right poison, no one would know.

Joe put forth his best effort and worked harder than he ever had in his life. He had to get this job. For him, having found the best spot in the plant was a wondrous event in and of itself, but it didn't stop there. When he reported his findings to Chandra, Joe had another suggestion, one that Melchior would be able to use no matter where he worked.

# CHAPTER 21

# First-Degree Murder

---

**April 2024 Near Tracy, CA**

By all estimations, Taylor was a good man. Most anyone around him would have attested that he was a model neighbor who liked to keep to himself. He was married, had two kids, and kept his yard on the edge of town spotless. His neighbors could count on seeing him every Monday, Wednesday, and Friday jogging his seven-mile loop, during which he would always stop and pet Sally, the Freedmans' dog. Perhaps he was a little too flirtatious in speech and stood a bit close when addressing his female neighbors, but he really was a credit to the community—essentially flawless.

Taylor excelled professionally as well. He held a prestigious title, one that he managed well: VP of Marketing and Technology. He had attained this position by working hard as a mechanical and electrical engineer. Over the course of six years, he had climbed to the top of operations and engineering at a midsized forklift company. When he found no other place to go in his career, he went back to get his MBA. With a few more skills in his belt and a lot of charisma, he was placed at the head of both the marketing and engineering departments at a much larger tractor and combine corporation. Most of his peers believed that within a matter of three to five years he would be CEO.

Home life was also good for Taylor. His two boys adored him. They saw nothing but good in their daddy and wanted nothing more than to be just like him in every way. He showered them with toys and gave them special presents every time he missed a soccer game or piano recital. He was a good dad.

His wife, Natalie, was a devoted woman whose main goal in life was a family that would stick together. She was proud to have a strong, good-looking man who was so successful. She admired how, even when he did not attend the boys' major events, he made it a point to repay the debt. She was as true as could be to her husband and children, and in many ways she felt fortunate. But she was the only person in the world, or so she thought, who knew that her husband had some flaws.

Taylor had a strange interest in India. Every morning, he would get ready for his day at work by going through the emails he had received in the past ten hours, and he would send quite a few of his own. Then, for a couple minutes, he would Google things about India, usually pictures of beautiful Indian women.

Natalie was not ignorant of his fascination with India. She knew he had visited it, but she could not figure out why he spent so much time researching it. She also was not ignorant of the fact that he often was looking at pictures of Indian women. She hoped with all her heart that he was not looking at Indian pornography. From what she could tell, that was not the case, and so she did not say anything about it.

Then she had an idea: *Why don't we take a trip to India as a family?* She pitched the idea to Taylor, but he was uninterested. "I know I spend too much time looking up things about India," he said. "But it's not somewhere I want to travel again. It's beautiful in its own right, but it can also be a rough and dirty place."

"Then why do you spend so much time obsessing over it? I see that a lot of what you're looking at is women," Natalie asked, scared of what the response might be.

Taylor was ashamed. He knew it would break her heart to learn that he had a secret longing for Indian women, but he had been physically true in their marriage and had no plans to be otherwise, so he thought it best not to say anything. "I know. I'm sorry," he said with a helping of remorse. "How about this: I will stop altogether."

It was just what Natalie had hoped to hear. She went and gave her man a hug and a kiss and walked away. Taylor, however, did not stop. Could not stop. And his hidden obsession with Indian pornography grew much worse.

On May 27, 2024, Taylor was doing the same research that he did every day—the research that had been breaking his wife's heart for years, that was bound to corrupt his children's minds and make them lose confidence in the man they admired.

His home office was on the north side of the house and bordered a field about 150 yards wide. Beyond the field was the edge of a woods that was fairly thin with a shallow creek running through it. It was the perfect place to commit murder.

Chandra had acquired only two weapons while in America: a thirty-ought-six and a nine-millimeter, both of which he got from someone on Craigslist. Over the previous two weeks, he had easily cleared a way so that he could take a shot from fifteen yards within the woods, right beside the creek. He arrived about 3:00 a.m. and waited for the light to come on in the room, giving him a perfect shot at Taylor. He could have shot him in the head at any time, but he wanted the heart. The room was far enough away from the rest of the house that there was a chance, albeit small, that no one else would wake when the window shattered.

Chandra was patient. He had practiced shooting several times off in the mountains. He could shoot a six-inch group from 210 yards. This would be a piece of cake.

It had been twenty-seven minutes. In three more minutes, he would end this man's life. Chandra was as still as granite. His heartbeat somehow remained slow, as did his breathing. Three minutes passed, and, like clockwork, Taylor stood up facing the window. Before he knew what had happened, the glass shattered in front of him and a small hole opened just left of his sternum. Nothing came out of his back; he had absorbed the whole load and fell straight to the floor. Taylor James Banks was dead.

Neither Natalie nor the children had known when they left the day before that it was the last time they would see their husband and father. And no one would ever know who killed him. Chandra followed the creek three-quarters of a mile, stepping only in the water, then shoved the rifle in the mud of the creek. He followed the creek another two miles to the nearest bridge, where he had previously stashed a complete set of clothing. There, underneath the bridge, he changed clothes, and then he walked onto the road clean, dry, and free of gunpowder.

Chandra enjoyed killing T.J. Before he pulled the trigger, he did not know what sorts of feelings he would have about killing. It is one thing to concoct evil plans; actually carrying them out is another story. But now he knew what it felt like. Even if the rest of the pain he lusted after didn't quench his thirst, he would be happy enough. His sister's death was finally avenged.

# CHAPTER 22

# An Unexpected Change

**May 24, 2024 HIllsboro, OR**

Everything was in place. Joe had been employed at Willamette Pure for almost a year and a half. Outside of work, he didn't really have any friends, but at the plant he had assimilated well enough to be one of the guys, albeit one of the weird guys.

That night they were going to produce a high-protein chocolate milk that would supply assisted living facilities throughout the West. It was a simple swap of sodium arsenate for sodium chloride. In all actuality, he was not sure that the dose was high enough to kill, but considering that many of the residents in these facilities would have weakened physiological systems, even a low dose of arsenic could be fatal.

He easily snuck the small amount of powder into the factory and took it back to the prep area where he could do his dirty work alone. He weighed out the powder to match what the recipe called for in salt, plus a little extra for bad measure. He wrote the correct weight on the bag along with the lot code from the real salt. Then he stared at it. This was it. For a moment, he hesitated, briefly thought about giving up. *Should I do this? All those people. Can I quit? No, no, what would Chandra say? What would he do to me?* His hands were shaking as he laid the bag on the pallet with the other ingredients.

He finished his shift and headed home for the night. Sleep, however, did not come as easily as he had hoped. His response to doing the deed was different than Chandra's. He did not feel good. He knew what he was doing was evil. He tried to tell himself that he was doing it for humanity's sake, but in such a matter as murder, solace was hard to come by. Even though it was incoherent, he found consolation in the fact that his poison was going to people who would have been on their way out of this life soon enough anyway. He was just speeding up the process a little. Also, depending on the person's body weight, what he'd done might not be that impactful anyway. Only a few people would likely die.

As with most anything in life, two things are constant in food production: change and surprise. This night was no different. The school lunch program put in an emergency order for more chocolate milk.

The production manager was scrambling to move the schedule around, and he sent one of his employees, Bill, to the back to prep ingredients. There was a relatively short window of time before they would need to re-clean the system, so Bill needed to work fast.

Among other things, this chocolate milk recipe called for cocoa and salt. On his way back to the ingredient room Bill saw the high-protein milk ingredients Joe had prepped earlier. The cocoa was the same brand as Bill's recipe called for. There was a little more salt in this recipe than in the other one, but if they left out the extra vitamins and minerals the protein beverage called for, it would be basically the same. He called his boss on the radio to explain the situation.

"No one will know the difference. Go for it," said the boss.

Bill grabbed the pre-weighed "salt" and cocoa, then sent them to the chocolate milk blender.

The next day, Joe was full of apprehension when he went to work. He would soon need to fulfill his second job. When he went to the board to get his assignment for the day, he saw that the pallet of raw materials he'd weighed out the previous day was gone, and today's assignment was the same as the previous day's.

"I already did this one yesterday. Do they need more?" he asked his boss.

"We had to switch things around a little last night, so it needs to be re-made."

A feeling of terror came over him. Getting the poison came at quite a risk to himself and the mission that he and his cohorts were on. If they threw the batch away, he would have to try again, and trying again could mean getting caught. "So they had to toss it?"

"No, your work didn't completely go to waste. The vitamins and protein are still in the back. They just pulled the cocoa and salt to fulfill a school lunch order."

Joe's eyes widened as he walked away. His head was reeling as he started for the ingredient room. It wasn't too late. He could say something, and no kids would get hurt. His hands were shaking and he wasn't walking straight. His stomach was ready to hurl all its contents onto the red-tiled floor. He threw his paper down and ran out crying and almost tripping on a couple of pallets. He could have done the right thing, but he didn't. Instead, he went straight home. He wrote a letter, duct-taped it to his stomach, then put a belt around his neck, wedged the end of the belt in a door, jumped off a chair, and within a few short minutes he had finished his second job.

Chandra would hear about it in the news six days later, when the chocolate milk reached to the first few schools. It crossed his mind to feel remorse, but instead a little smile came over his face. *Even better,* he thought.

Even though he was covering his tracks, he knew that it was only a matter of time now before he would get caught. There was only about a week until PFINE, and he expected to hear about Melchior's work at any moment.

Chandra made his way to his portfolio. He pulled out one of his more recent drawings and crumpled it up, then grabbed a new sheet of paper and started to draw two long tables.

# CHAPTER 23

# Blake Meets Joe

---

**May 29, 2024 DC/Hillsboro, OR**

*Children?* thought Blake. *Filth. This is low, even for terrorists.* Blake ran her fingers through her hair and put her head in her hands while she stared at the report on her laptop. Over the past sixteen years that she had been a special agent, Blake had seen people who could only be described in one word: *vile*. This, however, took the cake. This was pure evil. The scope was too big, and the target had been too innocent: Children. Schoolchildren.

*It's an inside job,* she said to herself. Long had the Bureau expected an attack, but no one expected anything this disgusting. Suicide bombs, shooting sprees, a gas attack, perhaps even poisoning food—but school cafeteria food? That wasn't on anyone's radar, which meant Blake would have to start her investigation from scratch.

She had looked forward to assuming the position of director of counterterrorism when she had taken it one month earlier. Now that she was in the midst of the most heinous terrorist attack in US history, she wished she were back at the embassy in Japan. She couldn't be blamed for negligence. In fact, all her peers admired her leadership, and the series of proactive measures announced during her first thirty days was unmatched by any director before or since. Indeed, an attack of this caliber had obviously been in the works for months if not years. But she would definitely bear the brunt of criticism, nonetheless.

After these brief moments of reflection, she got on her phone and called agents Thompson and Jeffries. She knew both men from field work in previous assignments, and prior to his retirement, Special Agent Frank Delfin had recommended both as two of his best men in the fight against terror.

On the phone, she said the same thing to both of them; "I don't care what you're doing, get in here now."

They came into her office a few seconds later at the same time. She was still sitting. They could both see that her mascara, which on any other day flawlessly graced her eyes, was a little smeared on the bottom and towards her ears from wipes finished before they each arrived. They weren't sure whether she had been crying or whether she had rubbed them in frustration. In reality, it was both.

"The information is still new, and not all of it matches, but there has been an attack. School cafeteria food has been poisoned, apparently with arsenic. Thus far, all the deaths have been in elementary school children."

A look of horror came over Thompson's face. "No ..." was all he could say.

Jeffries held his emotions in check as he inquired, "Is it isolated to one school?"

"Unfortunately no. There are five in the same area of Washington that have been confirmed to be affected. Police in the area are already demanding a freeze on all school lunches, and tomorrow the action will be nationwide."

"Are all the schools eating the same food?" asked Jeffries.

"No, they aren't," she replied.

"But they are probably drinking the same milk," he added.

"Bingo!" Blake paused. "And not all the kids are getting sick. I bet it's the chocolate milk."

"We're on it," said Thompson through gritted teeth.

"We all are," replied Blake. "Jeffries, we are on a plane in three hours. Thompson, I need you to control things back here. We'll get this guy. I'll send out the first communications to the Vancouver office and tell them to investigate the milk. Let's all keep in close contact. Get out of here."

The car ride home was a little longer than usual. She had the case on her mind, but that wasn't the only thing that was weighing down her spirits. It wouldn't be the first, the second, or even the hundredth time that Blake would have to drop the news that she had to go out of town immediately, but that didn't make it any easier. She hated every minute of being away from her family. Plans can be rearranged. To-do lists can be pushed out. However, kissing and hugging the ones you love, that was something that would just need to be given up for the moment. The only consolation she had was that the work was very important, enough so that people's lives literally depended upon it. Nonetheless, it was always hard, especially for the past four years.

When Blake came through the door of her garage in their Kensington, Maryland home, her four-year-old son, Blake, yelled, "Mommy!" and ran as fast as he could to give her his best hug and tell her about preschool. Her husband, Tom, stood back to wait his turn.

Blake tried to hang on to every word her little man told her, but her mind was elsewhere. When little Blake went back to his toys and Blake turned to her husband, she could see the worry in his eyes. She put her arms under his and up his back, resting her head on his chest. Her voice was low, distant, and forlorn. "I gotta go," she said.

"I know," was Tom's reply.

She looked up at him. "Is it already in the news?"

He smiled sheepishly. "No, I could tell in your eyes something was wrong."

How did she get so lucky as to find a man who loved her and supported her even when he knew it was stressful and took her away from time to time? "Something is *very* wrong. The worst thing that I have ever heard. It's a terror attack on children."

Tom pulled her in a little tighter.

"I gotta go to Washington tonight."

"That's not much of a trip," Tom responded, perplexed.

"Washington State," Blake responded.

"Ah, I see. How can I help?" he asked.

"Take care of little Blake while I'm away."

"You know I will. I have a trip planned to New York, but I can send one of my guys. How long will you be gone?"

"I don't know. Think you could have a warm bath ready for me when I get back?"

"Done."

Blake was heartbroken when she broke the news to her little man, but he was promised that he and daddy would do something fun while mommy was gone. She had only minutes to get her things together before heading to the airport. Airport food and long lines were already beginning to make her stomach turn.

She met Jeffries at the airport about twenty minutes before they were to depart. Departure was 8:00 pm and they would be on the ground in Portland at 11:00 pm. Then they made the quick drive to the Vancouver office and started to work. Needless to say, it was going to be a late night.

Blake needed to read some more emails and send a few of her own and so declined the idea of going to a restaurant. Jeffries went and grabbed a couple of fast-food burgers and fries and brought some back for her. "Take one. It'll probably kill ya sooner or later, but it tastes good," he said as he handed her a burger.

Without taking her eyes off her laptop, she took one, unwrapped it, and said, "Good thing I don't care about my health," then started to eat.

"I suppose we poison people one way or another," he replied.

Blake thought about the burger and little Blake. She thought about the massive amount of food that we consume and the massive amount of trust we put into the companies that produce it for us. She had no idea where that burger had come from, but she trusted that, at the very least, no one had intentionally put something lethal in it.

She thought about those innocent children, any of whom could have been her own. *Those little ones have full confidence in their parents, their school, and their cafeteria that they can eat what is put before them. Eating is such a basic thing. The safety of food should not be something that children need to worry about when they sit down at the dinner table or their school lunch tables. Unfortunately, much of the food we eat contains ingredients from several different states, countries, even continents. We simply don't know what we are eating. When it comes to food service, especially low-cost food service like school lunch, we know even less.*

She lifted her head. "We've got a big problem on our hands."

"I know. This is the biggest case I've seen yet," said Jeffries.

"It's even bigger than you realize. How do you know that burger won't kill you?"

A light came on in Jeffries' eyes, and he nodded in agreement. "I don't."

"You're right. None of us knows. In the past, we've been able to minimize threats to public health. We tell people don't smoke. We teach safe sex. Doing these things will greatly lower your chances of X, Y, or Z. We can't tell people not to eat. The poison kills you, and so does not eating. There are kids in the schools we will visit today whose only dependable meal is the one they get at school. Right now, they have been told they can't eat."

Blake paused to swallow a lump in her throat and extinguish swelling emotions of anxiety and sorrow that were making their way to her eyes. After a breath, she finished. "Let's just hope that it stops here."

When they got to the office, they heard the heart-wrenching news: 573 dead so far. About 115 kids at each school. The smallest ones were the hardest hit. Blood tests revealed that many more were poisoned as well but were able to weather it due factors like body mass, tolerance, and how much of the milk they'd consumed. About a hundred kids were still in critical condition.

Their suspicions were correct. Arsenic was found in all samples of chocolate milk at the affected schools. Tracing it back to Willamette Pure was easy, and production had already been shut down. Contaminated milk was found at six other schools, but those schools had more than a day's supply on hand and were not planning on using the bad lot until the following day. All of it was seized by the police. There was a little left in Willamette Pure's cold storage. That was the last of it.

Upper management cooperated completely with questioning by police. Re-questioning by Blake and Jeffries dispelled any real concerns that any executives were directly involved, but that didn't mean they would be off the hook.

Next in line for questioning were the managers and supervisors. By this time, those who texted or watched the news knew what had happened. The rest whose RSS feed was a co-worker were still in the dark.

By the time they got to Joe's supervisor, John, they still didn't have any leads. Everyone who was learning about it for the first time was shocked beyond belief. A couple of people even started crying. Blake hoped that, nestled in the tears, she would find the remorse of someone who had committed a heinous act, but instead she only found true sorrow. There was nothing.

In like form, John was shocked. Investigators didn't really suspect him since the milk had been made on the night shift, but they questioned him anyway.

"What kind of evidence can you supply us that would let us believe you were not the reason this happened?" asked Blake.

"There's no way that I would ever hurt anyone, especially a kid. I don't even know where I would get cyanide or whatever you said," he replied.

Blake believed him. "Nice try. It was arsenic."

"I really had nothing to do with this. You can ask my family, my friends, anyone. I go to church, I coach youth soccer. I swear, I did nothing."

"Well, everybody else is saying the same thing. Somebody's obviously lying," said Blake with as straight and disgusted a face as possible.

"I've known these guys for years. I just can't see any of them doing something like this. I mean, it must have come from the ingredient suppliers," John replied.

Jeffries was already contacting special agents and authorities in the areas of origin for the ingredients: cocoa from the Ivory Coast, vitamins from China and Europe. These efforts wouldn't bear fruit overnight. "You're ready to blame them, I see. You don't think anyone at Willamette could have done this?"

John scanned his mind as quickly as possible to think of anyone who could conceive of something so wretched. No one came to mind. "No."

"And no one that you know of has been acting strange lately?"

Right about the time he was going to give the same response again, a light came on. *Joe. He wouldn't...*

"You're thinking something," said Blake. "Tell me right now, or I'll put you under arrest."

"Joe."

"Joe who?"

"Joe Allen. The other day, he ran out of the building. He looked sick. He was about to go on vacation the next day, so I didn't think anything of it that he didn't come back."

"What happened before he ran out?"

"He was upset that he had already weighed ingredients for something we were asking him to do... Oh no... He had to batch it again because somebody took the salt he weighed up and used it in the chocolate milk recipe."

Blake ran out of there and screamed, *"Jeffries!"* He came running from another room. Next, she burst into the HR office and demanded, "Get me Joe Allen's address. Now!"

It was about five miles to the complex off Cornell where Joe lived. Four cars rolled in at once, and police officers and special agents wielding 357s and 9-millimeters emerged like wolves to take down prey. Every male in the area was told to drop to the ground and was asked if he was Joe Allen.

They got to his door and pounded on it, yelling, "FBI! Open up!" The police pulled out a battering ram, and everyone else waited with guns drawn while they broke open the door. Blake and Jeffries were the first two in; several more officers were right behind them. Blake noticed a faint smell and started making assumptions.

Kitchen: empty. Living room: empty. Bathroom: empty. Bedroom one: empty. Closet: empty. Bedroom two: empty. They kicked in the door to what looked like a walk-in closet, and there he was. Several days deceased, smelling horrible. Blake read the sign taped to his stomach: "I didn't know it was for kids." She slammed the door, screamed, and threw a lamp, huffing and puffing and not caring that she was disturbing a crime scene.

One of the officers said, "Well, I guess this is where it ends."

She looked at him coldly and responded: "I'm glad you're so confident." She looked at Jeffries and said, "Get working on that laptop. I'll call the phone company."

# CHAPTER 24

# Melchior Gets a Tip

**Summer 2023 Orem, UT**

Melchior had a leg up on Joe. Unlike his friend who worked at the dairy, Melchior was educated. He had a bachelor's degree in chemistry and from his junior year onward had always worked in a lab. Therefore, Chandra had far more options for places to put Melchior. Moreover, as a degreed chemist, Melchior would have access to more sensitive information. He went to Utah.

He and Chandra decided on a supplement company because, like milk, it would allow for penetration into several demographics. Old, young, healthy, sick—just about everyone consumed supplements. Utah seemed like the best choice because so many supplement companies were headquartered there, and after a long two weeks Melchior was hired at Simple Living Purity Supplements.

There is a very quick learning curve to become a quality assurance technician. The work wasn't terribly difficult, but it was fast-paced, and the training period was only one week. The QA techs had four main duties: perform inspections, file certificates of analysis, enforce good manufacturing practices, and test finished goods.

Melchior had a good technician named Darryn as his trainer. Darryn, like Melchior, was young and pretty easy to get along with, which made Melchior's false show of kindness a little easier to summon forth. Darryn had graduated about three years earlier with a degree in microbiology and a minor in chemistry, making him not only an ideal candidate for the job but also an ideal trainer.

On his third day of training, Melchior was plating some samples for microbiological testing. Regardless of the product, the standard tests were total plate count, yeast and mold, coliform, *E. coli,* and *Salmonella* spp. Melchior thought it odd that they did not test for more "bugs" than these. It seemed like a serendipitous potential point of attack. He asked, "Aren't there other things that could get people sick besides these?"

"These are the industry standard tests," said Darryn.

"Couldn't there be other bacteria?"

"Maybe, but these are the highest risk. For other microbes, we rely on our suppliers' COAs. And realistically with our products which have no water to help the bacteria grow, it's just not a risk. And as a general rule for the food industry, or any industry for that matter, if the government doesn't make you do it, and your customers don't require it, it probably isn't going to happen. Things only change when there is a problem, usually a big problem."

Melchior smiled a little and said, "Understood." Then he went back to plating, but his mind was thinking of all the wonderful opportunities he had for a microbiological attack.

Both he and Chandra practically salivated at the idea of agonizing deaths caused by a microbial attack. The problem was that getting the cultures would be too risky. It would be easier to just get poison.

Time went on, but opportunities for evil did not present themselves, and Melchior began to see just how difficult it was going to be to carry out his malicious plans. For one thing, he was never alone at work. Whether this was an effort to prevent the very sort of action he was contemplating or a measure to keep the lines running, he could not be sure.

However, he considered himself wise to not jump ship. He continued to look for opportunities in the plant with the hope that he would find a weakness somewhere, but much to his and Chandra's dismay, nothing really jumped out. After six months, he had come to the conclusion that he could either intermittently taint a few containers or he could sneak some poison into a partial bag in the back. Both would be very risky, and neither would have the impact that he and Chandra had hoped.

He kept working, biding his time and waiting for Chandra's cue to pull the trigger. But something quite unexpected happened when he got a phone call from Joe. He was surprised Joe knew his number. Chandra had made it clear that they were never to speak to each other, and thus their numbers had never been exchanged. However, Chandra changed his mind upon hearing Joe's epiphany. Rather than try to re-explain it to Melchior, he had Joe call him directly.

Melchior's first instinct was to wonder whether Joe was undercover and he and Chandra were in trouble, but he listened a little. He hung up before reaching their one-minute limit. Then he called Chandra, who eased his mind regarding Joe. The next day he called Joe back at the number he had called from.

"We don't have much time to talk, so here it is. Become a truck driver."

Melchior was smart enough to not dismiss anything at face value, especially if it had Chandra's approval, but he needed more information. "Okay, then what?"

"Kraft paper bags. Have you seen them?"

"I'm unfamiliar with the term."

"They are the big fifty-pound bags that most ingredients are packaged in. They're paper on the outside and sometimes have a plastic lining. Do you know what I'm talking about now?"

"Yeah, I see them all the time. What's your point?"

"They're made with a quick release drawstring, which is just cheap twine. If you carefully remove the string, you can open the bag. You put whatever you want in, re-sew the bag, and–"

Melchior finished his sentence. "Put the bags back on the pallet and make the delivery. Perfect."

"No one will ever know. You'll just have to practice a few times. Later," Joe said, then hung up.

An evil smile crossed Melchior's face, but a much more evil thought went through his mind. All his other, weaker plans were immediately tossed as the germs of wickedness multiplied in his head. He stayed with the company for now, but his reason for being there had changed. Where he once searched for an opening to wreak his havoc, he now only needed to acquire a few skills and find out a little information.

First, learning to unsew and re-sew the kraft paper bags would be easy. Since most workers just cut the bags open with a knife, he merely had to pull a few used bags out of the trash and practice removing the twine and then sewing them shut again. It didn't take long for him to become proficient.

Second, he needed to get a commercial driver's license which he could do in three months.

The third item of business was to find out who made deliveries to the factory. Unfortunately for him, the raw materials came numerous sources; therefore, there were numerous delivery services to investigate. Before he could reasonably decide where to seek employment, he needed to make the best possible choice of raw material to target. Having worked on the line and being well versed in what was made, he knew that much of what they manufactured became calcium supplements for the elderly, especially postmenopausal women. These supplements were widely consumed, and because tricalcium phosphate and calcium carbonate are both white powders, they were probably also the easiest ingredients to tamper with. Melchior zeroed in on the calcium distributors and was happy to find that all the calcium ingredients came from the same supplier, so he put in his application with the supplier's logistics company, and before he knew it, he was making deliveries to his old cohorts at the supplement factory.

The factory kept a rotation of tricalcium phosphate on hand that would last about two weeks. In order to time it for early June, he would have to make his delivery about ten days or so before Joe carried out his job. This would allow him to hear the news and do his second job before Chandra finished up the deal at PFINE.

By mid-April, he knew he had to take his next opportunity. It came on May 19, 2024. He was scheduled to deliver a few pallets of tricalcium phosphate to his old employer. He grabbed his work bag containing ten pounds of sodium arsenate and headed out for what would surely be his last trip from the distributor in Colorado to the Utah Valley.

It was 2 a.m. He had already driven more than six hours, and he was nearing Evanston, Wyoming. He had made the drive several times over the past year. He pulled off the interstate to go to an empty fairground he had scoped out a few months prior. It was on the outskirts of town, and its huge parking lot made it easy to maneuver and gave him plenty of privacy even if other were to come in.

Trailers loaded with a single food ingredient were usually locked before the driver's arrival, to be opened only by the recipient. However, this trailer contained a mixed lot of materials and had no lock. He opened the doors and entered the back with his work bag. He removed some of the stretch wrap holding the pallet together and grabbed a bag off the top layer. His fingers worked methodically as he carefully removed the drawstring, just as he had practiced so many times before.

It was the first time in months that he had seen tricalcium phosphate up close, before it gets shaped into a pill with other ingredients. It didn't look like what he had to replace it with. The calcium was very finely ground and clumped. The arsenate was a crystalline powder, like salt. Ideally the arsenate would have been more finely ground or the poison would have been something different, but it was too late for either of those. He removed part of the contents of a bag, added the arsenate, and mixed them together. Much to his delight, you couldn't tell twenty percent of the bag was something else. Then, stitch by painstaking stitch, he carefully sewed up the bag. He replaced it on the pallet and rewrapped the whole thing. It looked like nothing had happened. *Nice work, Joe*, he thought. A curious deer had come to see what was going on. Melchior looked at it and, with a soft chuckle, said, "Don't tell anyone, okay?" Then he continued on his journey.

On May 18, 2024, a day early, the drop-off went without a hitch. From there he went to the Salt Lake office, dropped off the truck, and resigned. When asked what he was going to do, he said he was going to take a flight back to New York. Then he started walking south. His plan was to walk and stop occasionally at restaurants to watch the news. Once he saw that his first job had been completed, he would go to a police station, yell out his guilt, and there die from the arsenic he'd saved for himself.

Now, he had only to walk and wait.

# CHAPTER 25

# A Pleasant Surprise

**May 31, 2024 HIllsboro, OR**

Blake stared down at her watch, wishing it had the wrong time and the wrong time zone. Images of Joe hanging with the note taped to his body kept coming back to her mind. *Coward. As if that stupid note could make a difference,* she thought. If he had felt that bad about it, he could have at least given them more information. And, though she had no real leads, she could easily see that Joe had covered his tracks.

Though she did not yet know of Chandra Sandeep, his garb of secrecy was plain as day in the files she was reviewing. His plan to keep all phone conversations under one minute was good, but what made it even better was that he, Melchior and Joe all made phone calls every day to people they didn't know. These, too, were generally under a minute long. All summed up, there were almost a thousand seemingly unrelated numbers Joe's phone had called, most of them called multiple times. Blake had never felt such a powerful urge to break someone's jaw as she did right then as she looked at the list over and over, trying different search criteria to come up with something. She knew there were others behind this. She ripped up one of her printouts and let a yell of frustration rip the air around her.

Emails weren't much help, either. At first glance, it appeared that Joe sent few emails and received only spam. There were thousands of emails with subject lines about princes who had just inherited a fortune and great deals on erectile dysfunction meds. If there were any useful messages there at all, they obviously used code words that were going to take more time and expertise to crack than she had.

Except for the corpse hanging in the closet, nothing in the house had been out of the ordinary. There were no clues. The laptop was sent to Hoover for more in-depth evaluation, and Blake and Jeffries planned to spend the next week interviewing people.

Because Joe didn't have any real friends, the interviews of Joe's work associates went quickly. Blake was good at prodding, but very few knew more about Joe than his first name, and no one had seen him do anything out of the ordinary on the day of the attack.

On the third day of interviewing, still with no leads, Blake got a phone call from her boss, who had just finished speaking with the Utah County Sheriff's department. He gave her a brief synopsis and told her to read her email for the details.

She immediately opened the debrief.

That morning at 10:22, an employee of a supplement company in Utah had noticed a higher-than-normal rate of broken pills on the production line. Normal protocols were followed: broken pills were sent to a bin to be crushed and reworked into another batch later, while a few samples were sent to QA.

The quality manager noticed large white crystals in the broken pills and immediately ordered ICPAES analysis despite groans and protests from production that the correct products and lots had been used.

*Good for her,* thought Blake as she continued to read.

The emission spectrum revealed arsenic.

*Another arsenic job?* Blake sat up straighter in her chair.

The technician who detected the arsenic called the QA manager, who immediately ran to the floor, stopped all the lines, and ordered all the doors to the facility to be locked until law enforcement arrived.

*I wish it was always like that,* mused Blake.

Interrogations started immediately, and the gloves of all employees were tested. The only ones who had any trace of arsenic were those in the line of discovery, starting with the first person on the line all the way to the technician in the lab.

Next, the ingredient bags were tested. One bag of tricalcium phosphate was found positive for arsenic. Upon further inspection, it was determined that the bag had been skillfully tampered with in a manner that made it indistinguishable from the other bags.

Blake was relieved that no one had been hurt in this case. Her next step was to look for a link between this case and the Willamette arsenic case. It was harder to isolate from the milk, but after a few hours testing confirmed that they were both sodium arsenate. Her instincts about the Willamette case appeared to be correct. Joe Allen had not worked alone.

# CHAPTER 26

# An Unexpected Guest

**June 1, 2024 Davis, CA**

When Chandra saw the news that his modified supplement formula had not passed QA at the supplement factory, he was furious. He gathered everything he needed—one gun and a few snacks—into a small duffle and went to bed. He spent the entire night punching his pillow, crying, and trying to mentally plan for anything that could possibly go wrong to destroy his last attack and final showdown.

The next morning, he was ready to leave the house for the last time, but there was another big problem, Rita unexpectedly arrived at Chandra's door. Even though they had seen each other the day before like always, she was missing him, and since he had been acting particularly strange over the past few days, even for Chandra, she paid him a surprise visit. When she arrived, Chandra began to tremble.

Although she knew that he would say no, she asked if she could come in. A million thoughts went through Chandra's mind. In his rage, he had forgotten about Rita. He wished with all his being that he could forget her again, but there she was. He knew that his life would soon be over, and suddenly a part of him did not want it to end, and that was because of her. He had conflicting urges to puke and sing with joy at the same time.

With his hands shaking, he invited her in. His frenzied mind was weaker now than it had been in a long time. He was breathing heavily. Rita shut the door and noticed just how nervous he was. She pulled him in and hugged him.

He turned and headed to the bathroom and shut the door behind him. His heart was racing so fast he thought he would pass out. His breathing was deep and uncomfortable. *She shouldn't be here*, he thought. How could he get rid of her? He didn't want to hurt her, but there was no turning back now. He had to move forward as planned. How he wished that he had left earlier and never seen her! He stood there panting for a few minutes while trying to think of how to get rid of her without breaking her heart.

What could he do? What could he do? He loved her more than his own life, but he had to get rid of her. He knew what to do. He could do what he had wanted to do for months. He would go out there, put his arms around her, and put his lips on hers. It was what both of their hearts longed for. He could then promise her that they would see each other later that night. Then he would kiss her again and send her off. And when her heart was broken, he would not need to endure it. He would be long gone. She would see in the news what his ruin was, but he would not have to endure her agony nor get talked out of it by her. It was the perfect plan. He would...

Mid-thought, he remembered: *The portfolio!*

While Chandra had been worrying and contriving his plan, Rita had made her way to the hearth. There on the mantel, she saw a binder of sorts. In a clear pocket on the outside was a drawing that looked as if a child had drawn it, albeit a child with a talent for drawing. It was the piece six-year-old Chandra had done so long ago, before he'd become an only child. Rita saw the hands. She did not understand the meaning of the drawing but was moved by the sorrow in it. She realized then that this binder was an artist's portfolio. *So he is an artist after all,* she thought. Not being one to ask for permission for such matters as looking at pictures, she ventured to open it up.

She saw his sister portrayed in stunning detail—so much so that she would have instantly known her in an ocean of ten thousand Indian women. Though Chandra spoke to no one of Kalini, the resemblance in the cheeks and eyes were undeniable: this was Chandra's sister. She stood in profile. White pearls surrounded her matted-down hair. The net of pearls and her hair came together in a perfectly strung flat braid in the back. Her forehead and sternum had matching gold pendants. Her well-fitted dress was mostly red and completely satin. She was looking straight ahead at Dr. Smith, who was also wearing traditional Indian wedding attire. The background was simple. It contained the world Kalini had lived in: their little shanty in all its glory, and Dr. Smith's office, above which showed a setting sun.

Had that been the entirety of the painting, this perhaps could have been a present for Dr. Smith. But there was more. In addition to the gold that graced Kalini's neck was a rope. Three faceless figures, one pale-skinned and two dark-skinned, were holding the rope as if ready to suddenly yank. The rope itself was colored red, white, and blue.

Rita furrowed her brow, confused. *Interesting,* she thought.

Turning to the next page, she saw a dumpster which took up the center of a drawing. The dumpster was in front of an old building that was covered in grayed soot. All the buildings in the alleyway, which led from the rear, were the same. The only thing distinguishable on any of them were some words written in a language that appeared to be Asian.

Chandra was in the drawing. His arms were behind his back, and his wrists were in handcuffs. He was being escorted by a walking tuna holding a pistol. The tuna itself wore a thick, wide belt that was obviously the label for canned tuna. In a very small part of the belt she could see an American flag. Chandra's head was turned back. Rita could see tears in his eyes. He was looking at the ground by the dumpster. There lay a pair of legs with red heels on the feet.

The drawing didn't make sense, but Rita understood that somehow this was an event that had happened. These three pieces of art were illustrations of Chandra's history. She was getting her first glimpse of who he was deep down. She knew that continuing to turn these pages would allow her to finally break through the defenses he had put in his mind. She knew it was an invasion of privacy, one he would not welcome, but she kept going anyway.

Opposite this drawing was one even more perplexing. A large white duck wore a lab coat and a hairnet. The floor was concrete, and pipes and conveyors were seen everywhere; it looked like a factory. The most obvious conveyor was directly in front of the duck. On it was a body bag that had been unzipped partway to reveal a dead man's head. With one wing, the duck was shaving off the man's hair; with the other, it was tossing the hair into a hopper on some sort of machine with a dial on it which was set to BREAD. On another conveyor, emerging from the other end of the machine, was a loaf of bread that had written on it "Made in the USA."

The first few drawings had been strange enough, but this one took the cake. Rita had no idea what it meant. The artwork was impressive. Though she could not understand it, the feelings it portrayed were strong. But beyond the themes of death, anthropomorphic animals, and a life marred with sorrow, she could make nothing of it. There was one other theme, she realized: disdain for America. Rita was worried but intrigued beyond measure.

She turned the page. There she saw herself. Chandra's detailed hand portrayed her face with a precision rivaled only by the mirror. Her hair was depicted with a wave that she normally would not have taken the time to style, but she had to admit it looked good on her. But more than her hair, her attire was completely different from anything that Chandra had ever seen her in. She was wearing a solid black spaghetti-strapped dress covered in sequins, its bodice form-fitting enough to reveal a few of the curves of womanhood without exaggeration. From the hips down to the hem, which was just below the knees, the dress hung of its own accord with a wavy pattern about it so that if she were to spin, it would have plenty of room to billow out. On her feet she wore heels that that were sequined and the same color as the bodice of the dress.

Chandra was also in the drawing. In fact, his mouth was connected to hers; they were passionately kissing. This brought a smile to Rita's face. It was the relationship she wanted and longed for: her Chandra in her arms. She would gladly give herself to him. The picture gave her hope. However, her smile did not last long.

She looked more closely at her arms. They were wrapped around Chandra with the elbows down, which is why her first inclination had been that she was using her might to pull him in. But she was wrong. Her hands met in the middle of Chandra's back, and they weren't empty. She had a knife, and she was thrusting it into Chandra's heart.

She looked back at the faces. Chandra's eyes were closed. She had seen this earlier but thought they were closed in the rapture of a kiss. Now it was obvious: he was dead. *Why?* she thought. *What would possess him to draw me like this? He knows I would never hurt him.* She turned the page.

The next drawing was different from the rest: she understood it. Chandra was standing amid four rows of tombstones. Every tombstone had the same date on it: May 29th, 2024. As the graves receded into the distance, they gradually became cafeteria tables, complete with school food on trays, and the tombstones themselves became children. She looked closely at the tombstones. None of the birth dates was before 2014.

In this drawing, Chandra's face was turned down slightly. He wore a devilish grin and had a tear on his cheek. In his left hand, he held a standard gable-top pint milk container. It was leaking, but it was not leaking milk. It was blood.

*No!* she thought. *It can't be!* Everyone knew that the milk terrorist had committed suicide. Chandra could not have been him. Deep down, however, Rita sensed Chandra was involved somehow. For a moment she thought she should run, but, stupid as it was, her desire to talk to Chandra and get some answers caused her to turn the page instead.

Next, she saw Chandra dressed in a lab coat with a stethoscope around his neck. He was behind a counter, and foreground of the image was filled with elderly people. On the counter itself lay several open pill bottles and a large pile of pills. He had just thrown a handful of the pills into the crowd so that about half were still mid-flight. The other half were either on the people or close to them, but all of these had gone through a metamorphosis. Instead of pills, they were now scorpions. and what, at a quick glance, might have appeared to be a few short people clamoring for a pill were in fact a few individuals screaming and falling to their deaths.

On the way over, Rita had turned on public radio and heard that some arsenic-laden supplements had been found in a factory in Utah. The pieces clicked together. *Chandra's the mastermind. Why did I try so hard?* She had to get out of there immediately. She turned around to run.

Chandra was standing there with a gun. Their hearts were both racing. Rita was trembling. Chandra's eyes were wide and his face was sweaty. He started to cry. "I told you," he sobbed. "You don't know me!" Even though he would never let her get in the way of his work, he couldn't bring himself to kill her.

He lifted the gun and pointed it at his own head. If she had not been so compassionate, she would have either stood still or tried to run, but Rita was true to herself. "Don't!" she screamed in agony as she yanked down on his arm. A bullet went right under her chin and out the back of her head. Chandra let out a bloodcurdling yell. Rita dropped to the floor and writhed briefly as blood gushed out of her throat. Her eyes looked at Chandra one final time. She didn't smile, nor did she frown, and she was unable to say anything. Then her spirit left.

Falling to his knees, Chandra let out a piercing shriek. He may have been crazy before, but now he was mad with bloodlust. The deaths he couldn't prevent—Kalini, their parents, the woman from the bar, his shipmate—had left scars that no amount of time would heal. This time, he was the cause of death. Rita was the only person in the world who still meant anything to him, and he had just shot her in the head. He blamed America.

Chandra was dead. His heart was beating, his mind still worked, but there was no more Chandra. He was already gone. He would finish up some business and get out of this life. He kissed her forehead, then grabbed her cell phone, his cell phone, and his laptop and drove away. In his maddened rage, he forgot about his portfolio.

# CHAPTER 27

# THE HUNT

---

**May 31, 2024 HIllsboro, OR**

As soon as Blake finished the email, she immediately called Jeffries and told him to meet her at their car to discuss something private.

"More arsenic. Utah," she said.

Jeffries' eyes rolled and he slumped forward and rubbed his eyes and forehead. *This is a nightmare,* he thought.

"But I received one piece of good news."

"I don't see how," he said.

"No one got hurt."

"Really?" replied Jeffries.

"Yeah. It was an attack on supplements, but the pills didn't form right. They had them analyzed and found the arsenic."

"That's amazing. I wonder why that didn't happen here," said Jeffries.

"It's probably just the nature of the business. There was nothing about the chocolate milk to tip them off like that. Mineral supplements, that's another story."

"True enough. So, are we headed out there?"

"Not yet. We need to make sure to wrap things up tight here before we move on."

It was a level-headed decision but a commitment that she would not be able to keep. A few days later, she received a call from the San

Francisco office. What had originally seemed to be a completely unrelated homicide had turned out to be a huge clue into the case. A PhD student by the name of Rita White had been found shot to death in her boyfriend's studio rental. Everything in the room seemed undisturbed, which indicated that there had been no struggle. There was, however, an open portfolio found near the fireplace containing artwork that depicted the recent terror attacks. The special agent in charge said he would take pictures and email them to Blake.

"I'll be looking for them," she said.

"Looking for what?" inquired Jeffries as Blake ended her call.

"I think we may have our mastermind."

Stunned, Jeffries asked, "They already got him?"

"Unfortunately not. He murdered his girlfriend and left some drawings or something. San Francisco is going to send them." She looked down at her phone. "And here they come."

She and Jeffries looked over the pictures. "Who is this guy?" he asked.

"His name was Chandra Sandeep, but who he was is exactly what we need to find out. Get all the information you can." Blake stared longer at the last picture in the portfolio, one Rita hadn't seen. "What do you make of this one?"

"Nothing, really, except that it's the strip in Vegas." he said.

"I think it's another attack, except that this one hasn't happened yet. It's different, though. The others were targeted towards groups of people." Blake paused a moment. "Children," she said, wincing. "The elderly. But here, it's just vendors on the strip selling hot dogs."

"Don't suppose he has a thing against street vendors, do you?" asked Jeffries, half joking, half serious.

"Maybe he does. Or maybe he already has plans to poison hot dogs that will be sold to vendors."

Much to Jeffries' chagrin, that hadn't crossed his mind, but it made a lot more sense than what he'd said. "I'll contact all the major hot dog manufacturers and tell them to test their hot dogs for arsenic. If any are in Las Vegas, I'll tell them to stop production until they have been tested."

"That's a start, but all hot dog manufacturers, not just the big ones, need to be tested. For all you and I know, hot dogs sold in Vegas come from Germany. And don't forget to find out who this Chandra Sandeep is. His other drawings are so abstract, we might be way off. Either way, we are going down to Vegas tonight."

Jeffries let out a sigh. Going to Vegas with his boss didn't sound like a good time. His lack of sleep and the stress of the past few days were wearing him down, and he missed his wife.

Blake didn't show it, but she too was getting worn out. She thought about little Blake a lot, and every time she got a few hours' sleep, she hugged her pillow and made believe for a moment that she had her little boy in her arms. Seeing that the plans laid for the previous two attacks had been thought out well in advance, Blake wasn't sure that the poisoning she hoped to stop was not already complete and on people's plates. She called her husband and told him not to eat any hot dogs for a while. He dutifully agreed and told her how he loved her and how proud he was of her hard work. The last few words brought a few tears to her eyes, which she concealed. She expressed her love, hung up, and swallowed the last of her emotions before going back to the computer. She printed large copies of the drawings to take on the plane, and then she and Jeffries headed to the airport.

At the airport, Jeffries gave Blake a rundown on what he'd been able to discern about Chandra. "Apparently he had some bad experiences while growing up in India. His parents were killed in a hit-and-run when he was young. Later, his sister died from an infection. Apparently, her infection had come from a wound inflicted by an American. He was never charged with any crime, but he was murdered at his home recently. Surprise, surprise."

Blake's eyes scanned over the artwork in her hand. As angry as she was at this young man she only knew by name and picture, she couldn't help but admire the artwork. One look at the eyes and cheeks of the woman in the painting revealed who she was. "This girl with the rope around her neck must be his sister. They must have been close if they lost their parents. So he decides to take out his frustration on thousands of other Americans," she said. "I also notice that most of these drawings have some sort of reference to the US in them. He might have had more than one beef with Americans." Blake flipped from one picture to the next, wondering what on earth had happened to this young man that would have led him to express himself in such disturbing art and get revenge in even more horrid ways.

"Yeah, the boys back at headquarters are looking into it, but so far nothing. Apparently, he was kind of a loner. Students who knew him said that the only person who really spoke to him was the young woman who is dead."

"I wonder why he singled her out," posed Blake.

"She's the girl stabbing him in this one. Police seem to think that she saw the pictures he drew and he had to get rid of her."

*Yeah, but she is stabbing him,* Blake thought. "Perhaps." She looked again at the last image and held it up for Jeffries. "We've got to figure out the meaning of this before it's too late."

"Sure, but it's late now. We've got to get some rest, or we'll be useless. Besides, the guys back home are working it."

Equally tired but more concerned, Blake said, "You can sleep on the plane. I'll be fine."

"Whatever, just make sure that I am the one driving when we get there."

They boarded. Jeffries put his head against the headrest and was out within two minutes.

Blake stared at the image of the Vegas strip for the next hour. "I know you're in there. What are you planning?" she mumbled to herself. She didn't want hindsight. They needed to figure out what was happening now, or more people would die—plain and simple. They were simply out of time; for all they knew, the dirty deeds had already been done. Nonetheless, she hoped against hope that they could stop this one.

With the intuition that comes from several years of chasing bad guys, Blake also knew there had to be more to the other drawings, something that could help her figure out the last one. Against the will of every part of her mind and body that was telling her to sleep, she wrote down every theme she saw in each picture as if she were studying for a test. A pattern appeared: fish, bread, milk, supplements, hot dogs. *What is his thing with food?* she half mused and half dreamed. *So, he is going to poison the hot dogs.* It seemed the most likely possibility, but there remained an emptiness inside that told her that she hadn't yet figured it out.

There was something else she hadn't noticed before: the vendors had gunshot wounds. The other two attack drawings depicted people eating food and dying. This picture was different: It was the ones who selling the food who were dying. *Maybe it's not the hot dogs. Maybe he's going after hot dog vendors.*

Blake felt like she was going somewhere with her thoughts, but her mind was turning off and her body was screaming that she needed sleep. She tried to focus on the picture, but her eyelids grew heavier. In a couple of hours, she would be on the ground again and would need to go back to work. *Huh... the bushes behind the carts and those two hot dog guys together look like the letter F.* She giggled to herself and was out for the remainder of the flight.

# CHAPTER 28

# Proceed to the Route

**June 1, 2024 Davis, CA**

Rita's blood-stained cell phone on the car seat was tormenting Chandra like Poe's tell-tale heart. His mind was vacillating as he stared at the car key in his hand. Who was responsible for Rita's death—was it America, the entity to blame for everything bad that had ever happened in his own life, or himself? He was about to put the phone under his tires and end its life, too, but amid his anxiety he had another idea to buy himself a little time. Sooner or later, people were going to look for Rita, and he would be suspect number one. With the clock ticking, he had to make it down to Vegas before she was found.

Rita's roommates were more like sisters than friends. He thought he would try his luck at texting them. He kept it short. He wanted as few words as possible so that they would perceive her voice—or, more accurately, not his—come through in the writing. He wrote, "Headed to the beach with Chandra, be back in a day or two!"

He could feel the vomit boiling in his stomach when he thought about what he had done to her. Worse, he was now impersonating her. It was all he could do not to pick up the gun and use it to end his own miserable life. He tried to find solace by lying to himself that it wasn't really he who had killed her; it was America, the same evil that had killed Kalini, his parents and so many more. He failed to see that, notwithstanding the injustices and problems in America, Rita, too, represented the country: her charity to the less fortunate, her love for others, her hard work, and her desire to understand the full picture. Chandra had never allowed himself to see that when Rita was alive, and now that she was gone, he certainly never would.

A minute after his text, the first reply came back. "OOOOh, have fun!" The sentiments of the others were the same. Their excitement seemed genuine, but he expected they would try to get hold of her again soon, even if she was on a romantic getaway. He figured he had two days tops, and that's if he was lucky. Before he started driving, he crushed the phone and destroyed its GPS chip.

# CHAPTER 29

# A Search for Clues

**June 5, 2024 Las Vegas, NV**

Fatigue is one of those things in life with an important physiological function that, when it occurs at inopportune times, we can find pretty annoying. It's great when we are at home tucked into our beds, but when we are trying to keep going on about ten total hours of sleep the past four days, and can't afford any time to sleep now, we dream of being able to turn it off.

Unfortunately for every college student, and unfortunately now for Blake, that is never an option. When she got off the plane, it was 5:30 a.m. and she could barely think. Her head was pounding from the rude awakening of an Airbus 320 hitting the runway that was still hot from the previous day in Las Vegas. Jeffries offered her coffee, but she decided to go with a Red Bull instead. Then she found a corner and started doing push-ups.

After one minute and forty push-ups, she walked back to Jeffries. It was pretty easy to see that she was in pain. He asked if she was going to be all right, knowing full well that, whether she was all right or not, she really had no choice but to keep working. She stared at him with a disgusted look and said, "Let's go." But like hunters in a new wood, neither of them had a clue where to go. They grabbed some more fast food and their car, then headed towards the Strip.

Like any day in Las Vegas, it was sunny, the air was stagnant, and though it was not yet 7:00 a.m., one could feel heat already starting to rise in the valley, surrounded as it was with mountains of glass. Except for homeless people and business-card-sized offers for illicit sex, the streets were barren, a stark contrast to the multi-billion-dollar industries that surrounded them and the rush of people that would emerge around 10:00 a.m. and continue until about 2:30 a.m.

# CHAPTER 30

# Chandra and Melchior

---

**June 5, 2024 Las Vegas, NV**

About one hour into his drive, he got a phone call from Melchior, who was as livid as Chandra about the failed attempt with the supplements. Melchior had decided to postpone his second job to assist Chandra at PFINE. Chandra was upset at Melchior's obvious lack of credibility as a terrorist, but he was glad for the help, and considering they would both probably be dead soon, he saw no reason to take anything out on Melchior.

Melchior had gotten to Vegas by bus about a day and a half before Chandra. Chandra had planned every detail of his attack as a one-man operation, but now that he had a wingman, he needed to rethink things. Therefore, he decided to postpone his attack until the second day of the expo.

Each had a .38 semi-automatic pistol as their only weapon. The first thing they needed was more ammunition, much more. They split up and visited two different retailers, both big-box stores, and readied themselves with one hundred rounds each. All the ammunition and both guns went to Chandra.

During Chandra's initial planning stages, he thought it would be perfect if he could somehow kill the lights. The lack of natural lighting at the expo center would virtually throw the room into complete blackness.

He found that the only way to cut power and ensure no emergency lights were activated was to go to the main control room. From there, he could make a run for it, killing a few workers on the way, and he would have a chance against the security guards. Otherwise, being outnumbered, it was a long shot. Furthermore, killing just the employees in the halls didn't really do anything for him. He wanted the main show floor. That was where he could really do the most damage. He had made all the preparations to cut the power, but about two months before the show, he abandoned the idea because it was too risky. However, with a second person, it would be flawless.

# CHAPTER 31

# Epiphany

**June 5, 2024 Las Vegas, NV**

Blake finished her delicate mixture of gray-colored meat, fat, spices, and phosphates meticulously formed into a patty nestled between two discs of white flour, hydrogenated oil, and baking powder. Then she looked up and saw perhaps the world's largest derrière graced with a feather tail and said, "I hate Vegas."

"Yeah, if you have tons of money that you have to spend and no morals, it's great; otherwise, it's a pretty sleazy town," commented Jeffries.

"It wasn't always that way," she replied. Then, shaking her head, she looked at the last drawing again. It certainly looked like an F. She scanned across the photo and noticed two more distinguishable letters: I and N, undeniably in a row. Unconsciously, she said, "Fin?"

"What are you talking about?" asked Jeffries.

"F, I, N. You can read it here on the page. Must mean something."

"Maybe it is code that this is his last attack. Like fin in French."

With all the disdain she could pack into one quick glance, Blake turned and replied sarcastically, "Thank you, Mr. Linguist."

Yeah, that was pretty dumb, thought Jeffries, remembering that Blake was fluent in four Romance languages, including French.

"You might be right, but I just find it strange that an Indian in the US would use French to tell his story. I'm going to look it up."

She spent the next few minutes on her smartphone searching for FIN. She didn't come up with anything that seemed to be related to hot dogs, weapons, or even food. They soon decided that just driving up and down the strip was getting them nowhere, and Blake had had to wake Jeffries up twice, so they started walking. They kept mostly to the side streets to speak with street vendors, especially the ones selling hot dogs.

There was nothing strange about the hot dogs, and not everyone got them from the same supplier. It was now 11:30 a.m. and they had gotten nowhere. Every joint in Blake's body longed for aspirin and a bed to sleep in. It was hot, and people were in a hurry in all directions to get somewhere. It was like the entire earth was in commotion around her, and she had no idea what to do and she knew she was running out of time.

They were near the north side of the strip on the east end across from the Mirage. Most of the people on their side of the street were wearing name badges and heading into the Venetian. Through the crowd, Blake saw a man pushing a cart towards them. Though she expected no new information and her body said it was time to stop, she dutifully started questioning him.

Just then, Jeffries' eyes went wide and he said, "Give me the picture."

Blake handed it to him while she kept talking to the vendor.

"Processed food," he said.

"What?" replied Blake.

"Hot dogs are processed food," he said.

"Whatever," said the man pushing the cart, and he kept walking.

"So what?" said Blake, though she knew and respected Jeffries enough to realize he was on to something very important.

He grabbed her by the arm and showed her a bifold informational stand showing directions to the Processed Food Ingredient and Nutrition Expo. The logo for the conference had a lowercase 'p' at the upper left. The next line had the letters F, I, and N in all caps, just as they looked in Chandra's drawing. A lowercase e, right-justified, on the bottom line completed the logo. Jeffries held the drawing up, and, sure enough, the p and the e were there, too. At the same moment, they noticed that that very logo was on all the badges around the necks of the passersby. "It started yesterday," he said.

"Today is probably their peak," said Blake.

Their momentary feelings of triumph at this revelation were superseded by fears of carnage that could happen at any moment. Notwithstanding their pain and fatigue, they both sprinted for the Sands Expo Center as Blake called DC and Jeffries called the Las Vegas police.

# CHAPTER 32

# FROM WITHIN

---

**June 5, 2024 Las Vegas, NV**

It was 11:36 on June 5th. Chandra gave Melchior a pair of maintenance overalls and the clearance tag that he had gotten from an online sleazeball who sold access to hotspots for a premium on the black market. Then they parted ways, with Melchior going down the hall toward maintenance and Chandra heading into the expo hall. Without looking to left or right, Chandra headed straight to the back wall, assuming that if there was going to be a firefight between him and the police, he would be able to inflict the most carnage from a spot as far as possible from the main entrance.

On his way to the back, he carried his bag just like everyone else on the floor, but unlike the others, he was not carrying ingredient samples and brochures in his bag. He had with him the two .38 pistols, fifty rounds of ammunition in clips, another hundred and fifty for reloading, and a pair of night-vision goggles.

He walked through the rows of booths. Some people were laughing and some were taking notes, each hoping that they could justify their presence there and the hefty exhibition price with some new business. Chandra, with business of his own, went about the deal-making utopia more or less unnoticed, despite the look of disgust on his face. One or two salespeople standing near the aisle tried to welcome him to their booths. They felt the evil emanating from him, but their main feeling about it was disappointment that they hadn't gotten a bite. Whatever fear they felt was instantly forgotten as the next passer-by approached.

Chandra's heart was pounding, but his soul was hollow and unresponsive to the stimuli. He got to the corner of booth I-6. He looked at his watch. It was 11:43:07. He considered putting a smile on his face, but the thought was fleeting. He stood there, arms folded, for the next 1 minute and 38 seconds.

At 11:44:45, he put his bag on the ground. A young woman standing by the back wall had been watching him for the past twenty seconds. She had an eerie feeling about him, and she started getting nervous when he bent down to get into his bag. He pulled out the night-vision goggles and carefully fastened them on his head so that he could maneuver at will through what would soon be a pitch-black hall.

It all seemed so strange, not only to the woman watching, but to several other people who were starting to take notice of his odd behavior. It was 11:44:59. The woman was the first to see what he had in his hand. "Gun!" she wailed, and everyone turned to look. Then they were enveloped in complete darkness.

# CHAPTER 33

# A Peek Down the Hall

**June 5, 2024 Las Vegas, NV**

Blake and Jeffries made it to the Sands Expo security office in three minutes. After quick introductions, they explained the situation. The chief security officer, Dwayne Gilman, was former LAPD. He listened intently. It wasn't a complete shock; he'd always known that something like this was possible, but he'd hoped it would never happen. "Do you want me to call for an evacuation?" he asked.

"No," replied Blake. "If he's in there and we evacuate without firepower, a lot of people are going to be in trouble. And, truthfully, we don't know if he's on the show floor, or in the halls, or hidden somewhere else. We need to hold off on entering until the police get here. Then we need to spread officers around the floor so that if something does happen, we can react. In the meantime, let's all go to the main entrance and act as though we are just normal security detail."

"Good idea," said Dwayne.

Without the police, there were eleven of them, nine security personnel and two federal agents, in total when they got to the main entrance. It was 11:39. They took their places to await LVPD backup. A few exhibitors at booths near the entrance cast curious stares at them, but in general they went unnoticed.

Even though it was the best idea they had at the time, and it had come from her, Blake was too anxious to just stand there. She knew that at any moment something very bad was about to happen, and she just prayed that the picture reflected the plan—that is, that there would be a shooter and not a bomb. Against a shooter, they could at least fight back, but if a bomb went off on the packed floor... she didn't want to think about the outcome of that.

A set of double doors off to the right caught Blake's eye. Something about it was bugging her. "What's in there?" she asked Dwayne.

"It's a hallway, mostly for maintenance and housekeeping. There shouldn't be any threat there."

"You're probably right, but I want to take a look around anyway," she said.

"I can get you a contractor badge if I go back to the office."

I don't have time for you to go back, she thought. "Don't you have a master key or something I can use?"

Dwayne knew better than to give her that. It went against every principle that he had ever taught his men. But considering the seriousness of the case, and not wanting to leave his post, he pulled one off his ring. "Take this. It's good for any door in the entire place."

"I'm sure I'll be right back," Blake said, and she headed for the doors.

She unlocked them, walked through, and closed them quietly behind her. The hall went down about fifty feet, then intersected another. Thus far, she didn't see anyone. She looked at a map on the wall: Boiler, Laundry Services, HVAC, Main Electrical. HVAC and Main Electrical, hmm... I'll just take a quick glance. It was 11:41.

In order to reach the main electrical room, she had to pass the laundry. She peered in the door and noticed about ten people, all of them working. One man noticed her and made a comment in a flirty sort of way. "Well, today must be come and see the laundry room day."

Really? she thought, and with her own flirtatious smile she inquired, "Why is that?"

"Few minutes ago, some dude come in here. Said he was looking for the electrical. I think he was new or something. Never seen him before."

Blake's smile went away. "What did he look like?"

"Darker skin, like Middle East or something."

"From India, maybe?" she asked.

"Nah, he didn't look like Gupta over there," he said as he motioned to another worker.

Blake instantly started making her way down the hall while calling for Jeffries to back her up. It was 11:43.

After a couple more long hallways, she could see the electrical room. She also saw a man in what appeared to be a maintenance uniform getting close to the door. She yelled out, "Excuse me!"

He kept walking.

"Excuse me! Hey! Stop!"

He ignored her, went into the room, and closed the door.

Blake started running down the hall. By the time she got there, it was already 11:45. The door was locked. She banged on it while drawing her .357. "FBI! Open up!"

Nothing.

She thought she heard some gunshots in the distance. Oh no, there's more than one. She unlocked the door with her master key and kicked it open. She didn't see anything. She kept her gun drawn, ready for a firefight. Then the metal door flung back at her, hitting her shoulder and head.

The metal door to the head shook her, and mingled with her extreme fatigue, put her in a temporary daze. Before she could recover, someone had grabbed her wrists and slammed them twice against the other wall, making her lose control of the gun. She was pushed out of the room and put into a chokehold from behind. Under normal circumstances she would have been able to easily handle Melchior. But with him getting the jump on her, and her being so exhausted, she was not in her best form for fighting. And now that she was on the floor in a headlock, she was in a pretty bad spot.

Fortunately, it was then that she heard Jeffries yell in an unusually savage voice, "HEY!"

To evade Jeffries, Melchior dragged Blake backwards into the room, then locked the door. In those few seconds that Melchoir was moving, he let up his grip which afforded Blake just enough blood back to her brain to assess the situation. She grabbed Melchior's hair, pulled it hard to the side, and gave him her best open-fisted left hook. She landed it right on his nose. She reached down and pulled a small Browning pocket pistol from a leg holster. Melchior grabbed her .357, but before he could point it, he had two bullets in his head.

# CHAPTER 34

# The End of Chandra Sandeep

**June 5, 2024 Las Vegas, NV**

For about half a second, which seemed to drag on for eternity, the air around Chandra was thick with fear and silence. Most of the attendees were in a state of stupor, ready to crack jokes about the electrical outage. The jovial atmosphere, however, was shattered by the explosion of bullets.

Chandra followed the wall, then turned up the next aisle. He started by picking off those who were the slowest to get to the ground. After putting lead into a couple torsos, he started to run with the objective of getting through as many rows as possible without giving anyone the option of attacking him from behind.

Soon, everyone was hidden or on the ground. He looked under tables for crouched people. He shot every standee and partition wall in hopes of getting someone who might be hiding behind them. A rush of adrenaline went through his body every time he saw a person in the fetal position squirming about as a piece of lead broke a rib or burst a heart chamber.

The rush was unsatisfying, but it was the most real he had felt in the past few days, so he kept going. In the first seven seconds, he had made about seventeen shots and hit at least six people. During his rampage, it crossed his mind that he could reload and keep going; without the lights, he was more or less invincible. Then he really started to get excited and decided that if he had no challenge from the police outside, he would use the last bullet on himself.

He fired off two more shots as he was about to round the corner of row 6 to hit up row 7. He saw one connect and felt the same adrenaline rush, but he felt something else, too, something painful on the side of his head. His vision went black, and he screamed as he fell to the floor. He attempted to fire a couple more shots, but his main firing hand no longer held a gun. He quickly tried to pull around his other hand to fire at the force that had come over him. Then, instead of sending a signal to his forearm to pull his index finger, his brain turned off. Chandra Sandeep was dead.

# CHAPTER 35

# ALL CLEAR

---

**June 5, 2024 Las Vegas, NV**

Upon hearing the gunshots in the electrical room, Jeffries screamed, rage running through his veins, and raced to avenge his boss.

"I'm fine. It's over," Blake yelled. She told him to go back to the main entrance and provide backup, then willed herself over to a breaker panel on the wall. With her head still ringing from the door strike, the chokehold, and the cacophony of her own bullets, it was all she could do to focus on the seemingly hundreds of switches and breakers before her. Thankfully, everything was flipped to the right except one. The breaker labeled MAIN HALL POWER was flipped left. She flipped it back on, took a deep breath, and ran back towards the expo hall, mentally preparing herself for a standoff. Instead, she found Dwayne calmly and Jefferies not so calmly directing officers and EMTs.

"Suicide?" asked Blake in utter disbelief.

"Yeah," said Dwayne. "When the lights went out, it was pitch black. He went on a rampage and started shooting. There was really no one able to stop him with his night-vision goggles. He killed at least two and wounded about seven others. Then he let out a scream, fired one shot, and that was it. When the lights came on, he was dead. Guess he just flipped."

"Seems like an awful lot of orchestration just to kill yourself, but it certainly wouldn't be the first time something like that has happened," replied Blake. She hoped the whole ordeal was over, but at the same time it was hard to believe.

She turned to Jeffries. It was then that he saw her swollen eye from where the door had landed. "We've got a lot of work to do," she told him, "but if those pictures meant anything, I think the worst is behind us. Once things are taken care of here, we can go home." Even in her current state, a strange physiological mix of adrenaline aftermath and exhaustion, her mothering instincts were clear and poignant. She could tell Jeffries was upset, and she could guess why, but she asked anyway. "You doin' all right?"

"Sorry I wasn't there for you," said Jeffries.

Her instincts were correct, and she had already formulated her kind but firm response. "You did what you were told. What I told you to do. If you hadn't come when you did and got that guy moving, he would have killed me. Whether you think so or not, I owe you my life. We got the bad guy. Now we have to figure out the rest of the story," she said. And she meant every word, but she knew that, deep down, he still felt bad.

He replied unconvincingly, "Understood."

The next two days were filled with interviews and reports. Every time Blake came across an account of Chandra, she cringed to think of the children who had perished in the Northwest. She thought of her own little man and how devastated she would be if he were murdered. She also thought about the terror and panic that must have ensued when the lights went out as Chandra started wreaking havoc in the expo hall. She still wasn't sure why he'd shot himself the way he did. He had already proved himself devoid of morals. It didn't make sense that he would kill himself when he had free reign in the dark room. He could have killed dozens more people without the least bit of opposition.

The coroner who inspected Chandra's body before its removal mentioned one small piece of intriguing information. There was blunt trauma to the head and shoulder which was assumed to be the result of falling on his goggles after shooting himself. Could be, Blake thought, but she made a mental note to look into it when she got back anyway.

# CHAPTER 36

# What Actually Happened

**June 5, 2024 Las Vegas, NV**

The Processed Food Ingredient and Nutrition Expo was by far their biggest show. As a company, they had attended it for over twenty-five years, and Mateo had gone several times himself. In 2024, it was in Vegas. Mateo was not a big fan of Vegas generally, but he was a sucker for Cirque du Soleil. So, there was no question what he would be doing at night. Following the obligatory dinner, he took his biggest clients to a show with him.

This, of course, made his normal exercise routine more difficult, and though he would normally be happy to have a few drinks with his clients, he stuck to water in Vegas so that he could get up early in the morning to do some CrossFit.

It had been a good show. He had finally met a rep from an up-and-coming beverage manufacturer whom he had convinced of the benefits of adding vitamins to their juice. The quantity would be only about 9,000 pounds for the first year, but if the company's growth kept pace with its current trajectory, they would be using about three times that in two years.

He also contracted a few of their larger clients for the next twelve months, and though it was only June, he had secured his 70% bonus. Needless to say, he was feeling good about the way things were going.

It was getting close to lunch on the second day when a young man from a retail supplement company approached him. He was looking for a powder form of vitamin K2 that they could easily incorporate into a dry pill formula they had.

"Currently, all we have is liquid for K2, but I know we've been working on something. What's the volume on this project?" asked Mateo.

"Depends on the usage, I suppose, but..." The young man kept talking, but someone else caught Mateo's eyes. It was another young man. He wasn't wearing anything unusual, and he wasn't carrying anything unusual, but there was something familiar about him. It wasn't his facial features; Mateo was quite sure he had never seen him before in his life. It was something else, something you know when you see yet find it hard to describe. It was seething evil. It had been a long time since Mateo had seen it, but he had seen it before. He had fought it before. The last time he had seen it, the venue had been very different. He'd been quite a bit younger and had two legs then.

The look in this young man's eyes had taken Mateo so completely by surprise that he entirely forgot the conversation that he was having. Part of him wanted to reach for his 9mm and follow the man, but he didn't have a 9mm, nor any other weapon. He was a salesman.

He thought that he must have been daydreaming. He shook his head a little, then apologized to the young man he was speaking with. I must be paranoid, he thought, but he knew he wasn't. He had seen it before.

He took the young man's information and promised to call. He then looked in the direction that he had seen the Indian man walk. It was crowded at the moment, but he kept looking anyway. There was a quick break in the crowd. Night vision? he thought as he got a quick glimpse of Chandra. He heard a shrill cry—"Gun!"—and then the hall went pitch black.

He yelled out, "Get down!" He heard the gunfire start at the end of the row and could tell it was getting closer. His instincts went back to special operations. He headed toward the stairs of the booth and grabbed a couple of the metal water bottles PEN was handing out that year.

He couldn't see anything, but he could track the perpetrator's progress by the flashes from his pistol. Unless he made a sudden stop and turned around, there was nowhere for the shooter to go except towards him.

Mateo ran towards the middle of the booth and made quick work of the flimsy wall that separated the meeting areas knocking it down so he could maneuver more freely. The shooter was moving faster. He gauged the distance between the booth and the shooter and between his current position and where he would land. It would be difficult, nearly impossible, to land it properly without actually seeing him, and landing in front of the shooter would mean certain death. These calculations were going through his mind, not to mention the thought that he had never attempted a jump like this since he lost his leg.

Yet even the thought of breaking a hip on the landing or getting shot if he were too early meant nothing to him. He counted his life as nothing in the current situation. His family would miss him, for certain, but they would be all right. He had to stand up for those around him. A voice he had heard long ago penetrated his mind: For all you know, the world may need your help again.

It was showtime. He leaned back on his right leg, and then he ran from one corner of the booth towards the other, hoping to not hit the railing mid-flight. He jumped and touched it as he glided over. The shooter shot twice while he was gliding down. Mateo saw the flashes; he had overshot about a foot. With all the might he could muster, he swung the bottle in his right hand.

He connected. With a mighty blow, he struck the shooter on the side of the head, causing him to collapse and fall. The fall threw the shooter under Mateo, breaking his own fall. Almost instantaneously and without thinking, he went for the shooter's hand and disarmed him. As he felt the shooter moving his other arm, he put a bullet in his head.

Instinctively, Mateo would have put two more in as well, but that was the last bullet in the gun. He dropped the firearm and went back to hide at the PEN booth, where he stayed until the lights came on.

222

# CHAPTER 37

# AFTERMATH

---

Trust. The level of trust put in those who grow and make food is astronomical, and rightfully so. Only rivaled by breathing, eating is the most basic thing done in life more than once a day. There is an understanding that what is purchased at the grocery store is clean, nutritious, and, above all, safe. And when it is eaten there is no expectation of getting hurt.

This is especially surprising considering that, with rare exception, no one knows any of the dozens or even hundreds of people who have come in contact with the food before it is eaten. Consumers never see the animal. Consumers never see the plant. Consumers haven't visited the factory. In fact, no one even knows, and even if they tried to find out they could not know, with certainty how many countries make up the history of something so simple as a stick of gum—and that is to say nothing of what went into the pack that houses all eighteen pieces of gum, nor the individual wrappings around each stick. Even so, for the most part food in the United States is safe, but not impervious.

With Chandra dead, the sun had finally set on one of the worst—considering the victims, perhaps the worst—terrorist attacks in the history of America if not the world. And like most other horrible events in history, no one thought hard enough about how to prevent it from happening until the catastrophe hit for the first time. What makes matters scarier is that this is not anything that the government or food manufacturers hadn't considered. The threat had been there for years, but drastic measures had never been taken because nothing like this had ever happened.

But once it did happen, Congress decided it was time to start putting greater measures in place to prevent it from happening again. So, just a few short years after the Food Safety Modernization Act, a joint committee of the Department of Homeland Security and the Food and Drug Administration was formed to investigate potential threats and, with the help of the US Marshal Service, enforce new laws promulgated under the Homeland Food Act.

The first things put into place were standardized testing procedures that go beyond the normal microbiological testing that had previously been done. When the FDA proposed new rules about the testing of heavy metals in several agricultural products, there was quite an uproar from the food sector. In similar fashion to the uproar against pasteurizing milk, the industry promised these measures would cost too much and people would no longer be able to afford food. In an effort to quell the torrent of complaints, tax credits were put in place to blunt the impact of the added costs. Interestingly, the testing stopped at heavy metals while other well-known, well-studied, and pervasive organic poisons such as cyanide were overlooked. And, much as with pasteurizing milk, the new measures saved lives and did not cost so much that people couldn't eat and companies couldn't make money.

If the reaction to heavy metal testing was heated, the reaction to the next item was violent. The FDA proposed a regulation that no one in a food production facility would ever be allowed to work alone. Lawmakers and companies joined hands in outcry against this. In an effort to throw out the rule, the big players in the industry pointed out that this would be too much for the little guys, especially those startups that only have enough work for one or two. Lawmakers said that the rule overstepped the bounds of the law, more or less making food a social program. The

FDA listened but was firm, and much to the chagrin of both sides, the rule was made binding only for companies with at least 50 employees.

Next was tamper-evidence technology. All ingredient manufacturers had to implement non-generic tamper-evidence measures. Generally speaking, there are only a few different types of containers for food ingredients: bags, drums, pails, and trucks. For the most part, single-source trucks already have locks on them that have to be broken at the company purchasing the ingredient. Basically, the same principle was implemented by regulation for pails and drums.

From the time of implementation, all pails and drums had to have numbered seals that connected the lid to the rest of the container, and if a drum could open on both ends, then the same applied to the bottom. The tamper-evidence measures themselves could not be generic. In practice, this meant that pail manufacturers started making lids for five-gallon pails, with lot codes that were easily visible. These lot codes, and the number of lids used, had to match what was on the incoming paperwork for the ingredient, or it had to be rejected.

Considering that Kraft paper bags were a culprit in this attack, they got the worst of it. A rule was implemented that all Kraft paper bags had to be closed with glue. If they wanted to keep the bag easy to open, it had to have a pull tab put into the paper itself which would rip open the bag in a non-repairable way.

Of course, few packaging manufacturers had the equipment to produce this type of tamper-evidence technology. So billions of dollars were allocated to help companies upgrade all their equipment, with earmarks for anything that would be needed to support the new rules. And in most of the companies, this meant executive support for the purchase and a bonus to the CEO.

Lastly, perhaps the biggest change was that pallet wraps could no longer be generic clear plastic stretch wrap. Ingredient suppliers had to purchase stretch wrap that had an easily identifiable lot code, and a law was enacted that any pallet with generic stretch wrap or more than one designated lot code materials on it had to be reported to the next recipient prior to shipment.

Oh, what an outcry there was when the Homeland Food Laws were enacted! It was too hard. It was too much of a burden. It cost too much. It would not help.

Were they right? Maybe so, maybe not. At the end of the day, if someone wants to enact any mischief in any setting, they will find a way, but considering the public's ignorance about food, it was a pretty good place to start. After a short comment period, all the rules became federal regulations, and, as with most other new regulations, companies found a way to comply.

Did the laws make food safer? They definitely helped. But there were other factors that were just as important. Knowing the complicated food system of the modern age is not impenetrable, people started thinking twice about where their food came from and demanded that manufacturers take greater steps to ensuring food safety. So, they did and there became a marketing race as it were to prove who had the safest food. With this added layer of transparency, indeed food did become safer. As Darryn at Simple Living Purity said, "Things only change when there is a problem, usually a big problem."

# Epilogue

**June 12, 2024 D.C**

After a week of seemingly endless interviews and paperwork, Blake headed home. There wasn't any turbulence, but that didn't matter; she still couldn't sleep. The trip, however, wasn't without rest. For the first time in about two and a half weeks, she wasn't under constant duress or fear that more people would die if they did their normal three-a-day routine.

When she finally got to her house, it was 3:15 a.m, and she was filled with a potpourri of emotions as she saw a trail of rose petals leading from the living room back to a warm bath, just like she had asked. Half of her was moved with love for her husband. The other half just needed sleep.

She was surprised when she found that he was not in bed. He hadn't been in the bathroom, either, and for a second, a multitude of horrible thoughts flooded her mind. She went to little Blake's room to see if the little man was there. He was. And so was his daddy, snuggled up with him. One little boy and one giant-sized boy on a twin bed, one holding a teddy bear and the other holding the first.

She would gladly have joined them, but alas, there was no room. So she picked up the flower petals, put them on his pillow and, for the first time in a few weeks, she got four hours of uninterrupted sleep so deep that she dreamt of sleeping.

Yet, as good as the sleep was, morning brought another day and, like most, it was not a holiday. So, she smothered some toast with jam and love for little Blake and gracefully covered her husband's lips with her own, both of them burning with desire for each other. Then, she went to work.

Though the hardest parts were behind her, she still had quite a bit of work to do on the "milk terror," as they called it, and would for the next twelve months. She had quite forgotten about the fingerprint scan that she had demanded of the guns. Therefore, it was a surprise when Jeffries came in wide-eyed with the report.

"I'm not sure what possessed you to ask for this, but it's a dang good thing you did. There still may be one out there," he said.

Blake's heart sank, it was like a never-ending nightmare. A fourth conspirator? I thought I was done chasing these guys. Every fragment—for fragments of prints were all they could find—had led to one of three people, all of whom were dead. Now a fourth? She thought about little Blake and started missing him. She wanted to cry.

"So, the shooter's prints are on both guns. Those of his accomplice, the one you took out, are on one of the guns, the one that he was holding. But the gun the shooter dropped also has the prints of one Mateo Gutierrez."

"Another wacko?" she asked, grimacing.

"I guess so. What makes matters worse is that he was an inside man. He was actually working a booth at the convention when it happened, and by all accounts, it appears that before the shooter yelled out and shot himself, he was headed for Gutierrez..."

Blake was puzzled.

"And it's a dang good thing he didn't get to him, because he would have really caused some trouble."

While Jeffries paused briefly, Blake interjected, "Why?"

"Former Navy SEAL."

"Navy SEAL?"

"Yeah."

Blake cast Jeffries a dubious look. "I don't buy it. None of it makes sense. Someone with that kind of training could have still gotten the guns and ripped the place to shreds. We're missing something. Is his history violent or anti-American?"

"No, and this is the most interesting part. Apparently, he is a really nice family guy. He teaches a free martial arts class for women and coaches his kids' sports teams."

Blunt trauma. The side of Blake's mouth came up in half a smile. "The gun that shot the shooter was empty, right?"

Jeffries was unsure why she would ask this and cast his own dubious stare at her, slowly saying, "Yeesss..."

Blake was confident. "Well, I think we got our man. Where does he live?"

"Southern California. But I already contacted his work, and he happens to be here in town on business."

"Well, we should pay him a visit."

"I'll call the Marshals," said Jeffries as he started to make for the door, proud that he had helped get the bad guy.

Blake's stern reply stopped him. "No. We will handle this one ourselves."

"He could be dangerous."

With a look of exaggerated understanding, she said, "I'm sure he is, but we're both trained. We'll do fine."

"You did hear me say that he is a former SEAL, right?"

"Oh yeah. I definitely heard that, but I don't think you need to worry. There's one of him and two of us. Do you know where he is?"

Jeffries was scared. "Uh, I have his hotel."

"Call his boss and tell him that he needs to have a virtual meeting with him. That way we know he will be available to talk with us. Get Gutierrez's location. Wherever he is, we will be there."

Jeffries shook his head and did as he was told.

What a fool, Blake thought.

The meeting was set for 3:00 p.m. The sun was shining brightly on that mid-June day. A warm spell was pushing through so that the temperature was right around 92. Blake was driving and had the windows down. She was as calm as a lake at sunrise, with her hair blowing in the wind as they made their way towards the park where Mateo was to be. Jeffries was the opposite. His hands fidgeted, he checked his piece a few times to make sure it was loaded, and he mentally cursed Blake for her nonchalance.

They got to the park and saw Mateo sitting on a bench with his WiFi hotspot on so he could call in at the appropriate time. While Jeffries was readying himself for a fight in broad daylight, flustered that Blake did not want back-up, Blake decided to go to the hot dog vendor and get a couple of franks. Flabbergasted, Jeffries said he wasn't hungry and declined.

As they made their way toward Mateo, they both noticed what great shape he was in. For Blake, this brought some admiration and respect. She immediately knew that a scrawny college boy would have been no match for him. For Jeffries, this brought fear, and he immediately knew that he, himself, was also no match for Mateo.

Blake walked straight towards Mateo. She saw Jeffries get his hand ready over his firearm. She looked at him. "I'm disappointed, Jeffries. He's our man, but trust me, you won't need that." She giggled a little, shook her head and continued toward Mateo.

Mateo was looking at his computer on his lap. He'd had some trouble connecting but found success on his third attempt.

"Mateo?"

Hearing his name called, he looked up to see a well-dressed woman with a well-dressed man at her side. He also saw the badges around their necks.

"Yes?"

"Mind if I sit here?" asked Blake, sitting down on his right without waiting for him to answer. She started to eat her hot dog and with a small laugh said, "This is a really good hot dog. Have you had lunch?"

"I have", he replied.

"That's too bad. Man, this is good." As if nothing was going on, Blake stared off into space. "Well, it sure is a nice day," she said.

After a brief pause, Mateo said, "I suppose you want to talk about PFINE."

She looked at Mateo with a look of disbelief, as if it had been the last thing on her mind, but then she raised her shoulders and said, "Well, since you brought it up, sure. Why don't you tell me about it? Blunt trauma to the head?"

"Aluminum water bottle," he replied.

"Ahhhh. Aluminum water bottle," she responded, smiling. She shook her head, slapped her own leg, then took another bite of her hot dog. It took her a few seconds to swallow. Then she asked the million-dollar question. "I've gotta ask. Why did you run? If your fingerprint hadn't shown up on the gun, we would have always assumed suicide."

Oh, crap. It had taken some time, but Jeffries finally got it. Mateo had killed the shooter with his own gun.

"I think the SEALs get enough unwanted spotlight these days. We don't do what we do for glory. We do it for country."

Blake pursed her lips and nodded. "You know, fleeing the scene of a crime could get you in a lot of trouble."

Mateo's look betrayed uneasiness. He certainly did not want to get arrested for saving people's lives. He could tell that Blake wasn't angry, but he knew that she did want an answer.

"Yes, ma'am. I guess I'm just hoping for leniency."

Blake pursed her lips further, furrowed her brow, and said, "I see."

"Is there any chance that I can remain anonymous?" Mateo asked.

Blake let out a laugh and looked at Mateo. "Not much chance of that happening. You must understand this has to go into the report, and because of that, I will need a very detailed explanation from you of what happened, and a very detailed explanation of why you didn't stick around." Blake's eyes were wide and her eyebrows were high as she paused for dramatic effect. "However, once that is done, I will do everything in my power to make sure that you, and your family for that matter, are protected."

"Thank you, ma'am," he replied.

"Here is my card. I expect an email from you by tomorrow." Before standing up, she asked one last time, "You sure you don't want this other hot dog?"

"I'm sure."

Blake slapped Mateo on the knee a couple times and said, "Tell your boss thanks for the meeting," at which time, Mateo realized that his boss would not be calling in. Then she and Jeffries got up and started walking towards their car.

Blake was cleaning her teeth with her tongue and fingernails and maintaining a smile as they made their way. Jeffries was smiling, too. "Hey, everybody gets to be an idiot once in a while," he said.

"Fair enough," said Blake. "But that was kind of a big oversight, don't you think?"

"Okay, okay. What do I owe you to keep this a secret?"

"Oh, ho, ho, ho," she said. "This one is way too good to keep secret."

"Come on! I'll polish your shoes every day for a month."

"And you buy lunch for a week."

"Fine, whatever."

Then they got into their car. Blake looked at Jeffries and said, "You know, my husband has a lot more business shoes than I do."

Jeffries shook his head. "Bring it on," he replied, an
jokes, they headed back down the same road that ha
there, happy that it was finally over.

233

amid jibes and
brought them

Jeffries shook his head. "Bring it on," he replied, and amid jibes and jokes, they headed back down the same road that had brought them there, happy that it was finally over.

233